A Lone Pine Adventure
NOT SCARLET BUT GOLD

A LONE PINE ADVENTURE

NOT SCARLET BUT GOLD

Malcolm Saville

First published 1962
by Newnes Ltd
This hardcover edition 1992 by Chivers Press
by arrangement with
the author's estate

0 86220 891 2

© Copyright the Estate of Malcolm Saville 1962, 1990
All rights reserved

British Library Cataloguing in Publication Data
Saville, Malcolm
  Not Scarlet But Gold.—New ed.—
  (Swift Books)
  I. Title II. Series
  823.912 [J]

ISBN 0–86220–891–2

*To all Lone Piners
everywhere*

Printed in Great Britain by
Redwood Press Limited, Melksham, Wiltshire

Contents

Page

    Foreword 6

    The Lone Pine Club 7

1. The Letter 9
2. The Handsome Hiker 18
3. Seven Gates 29
4. Fire! 46
5. The Patchwork Quilt 60
6. Not Scarlet but Gold 69
7. "She Knows too Much" 77
8. The Cave 88
9. Jenny Alone 103
10. Enter Tom 119
11. Peter and David 132
12. Jenny Solves the Riddle 153
13. The Treasure at Last 174

Foreword

Even if you've never read any of the adventures of the boys and girls who founded the Lone Pine Club and who call themselves the Lone Piners, you'll find this story complete in itself. You'll soon discover that the scene is set in a real part of the country to which you can go yourself.

There really is a great hill – actually it is a long plateau 1,600 feet high – called the Long Mynd, and not many miles to its west, rising out of the plain almost like a curiously-shaped prehistoric monster, is the gaunt ridge called the Stiperstones. I have known these hills for many years and I can assure you that there is a strange atmosphere of foreboding about the latter. It is said that the outcrop of black, quartzite rocks on the summit known as the Devil's Chair, is one of the oldest parts of England – older even than the Ice Age – and it is little wonder that this desolate, neglected country is rich in folklore and legend. The Romans once mined for lead in these parts and even today, below the western slopes of the Stiperstones, you will see the ruins of deserted mine workings.

The best places from which to explore the Long Mynd with its gliding station, the State Forests creeping down into its beautiful valleys, and its ancient Portway along which some of the first men in these islands may have walked, is one of the Strettons – Church Stretton, Little Stretton or All Stretton. The Stiperstones are not so easy to reach, but you can go to the Minsterly by bus from Shrewsbury, if you're not cycling or going by car, or use Bishop's Castle as a centre for exploring this little-known country.

This then is the scene of this story, but all else is as imaginary as the characters. You'll never find, for instance, Peter's Hatchholt, or the farm called Seven Gates, or the village of Barton Beach, or Greystone Dingle, or Black Dingle, for there are no such places.

M.S.

THE LONE PINE CLUB

The Lone Pine Club was founded as a secret society at a lonely house called Witchend in a hidden valley of the Long Mynd in Shropshire. The first headqarters of the Club was a clearing, marked by a solitary pine tree, on the slopes of this valley. The original rules of the Club are very simple and are set out in full in *Mystery at Witchend*, which is the first story about the Lone Piners.

There are now nine members of the Lone Pine Club, but it is not usual for them all to appear in one story. The following appear in this one:

DAVID MORTON
Age 16. Is captain and co-founder of the Lone Pine Club. He goes to a boarding school and his home is in London.

RICHARD (DICKIE) AND MARY MORTON
David's ten-year-old brother and sister who are 'look-alike' twins. They are inseparable except when at their separate boarding schools.

PETRONELLA (PETER) STERLING
Just 16. Really the founder of the Club. Has lived in the Shropshire hills all her life and goes to boarding school in Shrewsbury. She has no mother and in the holidays lives with her father who is in charge of a reservoir called Hatchholt, not very far from Witchend. She is David's special friend.

TOM INGLES
A sixteen-year-old Londoner who now lives and works on his uncle's farm near Witchend.

JENNY HARMAN
15. Tom's special friend who lives with her father and stepmother at Barton Beach where they keep the local general store and post office. Jenny has lived in Shropshire all her life.

HARRIET SPARROW
12 years old. A Londoner who is a special friend of the twins – Dickie and Mary Morton.

MACBETH
The Morton's Scottie dog who long ago was made an honorary member of the Club.

The other members are:

JONATHAN (JON) WARRENDER
Only son of Mrs Warrender who owns the *Gay Dolphin Inn* in Rye.

PENELOPE (PENNY) WARRENDER
Jon's cousin who is living at the *Gay Dolphin* while her parents are abroad.

CHAPTER 1

The Letter

In the north of Germany, at the mouth of the river Elbe, is Hamburg – a great industrial city and one of the busiest ports in the world with miles of docks and a wind from the sea thick with the scent of salt water and strange cargoes. It is a busy, bustling city and a mixture of old and new, for the blocks of modern flats and offices have risen from the ashes of the port destroyed in the Second World War.

This story opens in Hamburg on an evening in early spring. The scene is a small living-room on the top floor of one of the huge blocks of apartments not far from the docks. The only occupant is a man of about sixty. His dark hair is streaked with grey, but although his clean-shaven face is worn and tired, his eyes are kind. He crosses to the window, opens it and looks down to the tops of the trees lining the cobbled street. He can hear the clatter of an approaching train and the busy hum of work on the docks which never stops by day or night. He, Hans Schmidt, has had little to do but work since his wife died a year ago, and when he has delivered the letter to his nephew Johann he will have no other interest but his work as a clerk in one of the shipping offices.

Suddenly his thoughts were interrupted by the ringing of his doorbell. Not a short, timid tinkle but the firm ring of somebody who expects to be admitted at once. He opened the door and faced his visitor – a well-built, handsome young man.

"You must by my uncle Hans. I haven't seen you for years and I had forgotten what you looked like," he said. "I'm Johann. I saw the advertisement you put in the paper. What's all the fuss? And what have you got for me that is so important?"

"Come in, Johann. I'm glad to have found you. It's a pity you've never let me know where you live – it would have saved me both trouble and expense."

Johann looked at him with distaste. "Where's my aunt? She always gave me a welcome, and I liked her."

"So did I," Hans said dryly. "She died over a year ago – about twelve months after your own mother. You should have let me know where you were going when you left the city so suddenly. We are the only two left of our family."

"I'm sorry about my aunt, Uncle, but where I live and what I do is my business. You don't have to worry about me nor I about you. I'm not doing so badly one way and another, but your advertisement said you had something for me on my eighteenth birthday. I hope it's money because I could do with plenty just now. Today is my birthday and I hope you haven't been fooling me."

The old man put his hand on the boy's shoulder and his voice shook a little as he said, "No, I'm not fooling you, Johann. I had to see you personally because I promised your mother that I would hand to you the packet I have been keeping for you since she died. It is from your father."

Johann flushed. "From my father! My father was killed by the British in the war. How dare my mother keep what belongs to me for so long? Give it to me now."

"No need for the two Schmidts to quarrel, my boy. I'm pleased to see my brother's son and I'll tell you everything when we've eaten. Go and wash and I will bring more food and beer. You can surely wait for half an hour after waiting for eighteen years?"

Johann had the grace to look a little ashamed.

During the meal Hans tried to make his nephew tell

THE LETTER

him where he was living and what he was doing, but could get no definite reply and no real response to his attempts to be friendly. At last the older man gave up the struggle and pushed back his chair.

"Very well, Johann. I am, I believe, your only living relative and if you won't give me your confidence I cannot force you to do so. I have a duty to perform on your eighteenth birthday and I must ask you to listen carefully to me before I hand over the packet I have been keeping for you."

"Must you keep on *talking*, Uncle Hans?" Johann interrupted. "Can't you just give me what is mine so that I can decide what to do?"

"I must keep the promise I made to your mother, Johann. If she had lived until today she would have told you what I now have to say. She entrusted this letter to me to pass to you on your eighteenth birthday and not before, because that was your father's specific instructions. Neither your mother nor I know what is in your letter."

"How did she get it? My father was killed by the British in the war. I cannot remember him and I only have a photograph of him given to me by my mother. She has never told me where he was killed or how. Why have these things been kept from me?"

"Perhaps the letter will explain it to you. Perhaps she told you that your father left Germany a few months after you were born and that she never saw him again? That's a long time ago now, Johann, but it is true that your father is dead and that he died for his country, and the letter I have for you was delivered some time later to your mother by a comrade of your father's. It was delivered secretly and your mother only told me about it some years later."

"But where was he killed? She must have known. Didn't this comrade tell my mother?"

"I don't think so, Johann. I am not sure that your mother even guessed what your father was doing for his country, except that he was engaged on some secret, important work."

Johann got up from the table and strode up and down the room. His handsome face was hard and set as he turned at the window and faced his uncle.

"Do you mean that my father was a spy?" he shouted.

"I have always thought he was sent on a secret mission. You knew that he spoke English brilliantly?"

Johann nodded. "So my mother told me. She told me that he particularly wanted me to learn English and to speak it as well as he could, so perhaps *she* had a letter from him too . . . ? I speak English well now. Very well. I have been to London twice and I speak it like an Englishman. I am very good."

Hans did not like his nephew's arrogance.

"I hope you are good, my boy. Your father, in a way, was fond of Britain and the British and I believe that he was chosen to be one of those brave men who were dropped there by parachute –"

"And shot as a spy!" Johann shouted. "That's what happened. Give me the letter, Uncle. Stop all this talk. Let me read it now."

Hans sighed, went to his bedroom and returned a few moments later with a grey envelope in his hand. "Here," he said. "You will see that your name and the message are written in English."

Johann snatched the letter, walked over to the window and turned his back on his uncle. Hans sat down and closed his eyes. He felt strangely moved as he thought again of his only brother. A clever, gentle man who had shown signs of a great future. The sort of man who had hated war and yet, because of his unusual gifts, had found himself caught up in it with special responsibilities.

He glanced again at his nephew, who had now turned so that the light from the window fell upon the letter he was reading. His handsome face was set and angry, but when he felt his uncle looking at him he said, "Why didn't my mother tell me about this letter? Did she know what was in it? Do you know? Why was I the only one not to know?"

"Your mother did not tell you about it because it was your father's wish that you should not read it before your eighteenth birthday, and you will remember that she died suddenly when you were away three years ago. I do not believe she knew the contents and neither do I. Are you going to tell me? Your father was my only brother and I am ready to help you if I can, for his sake . . ."

"I wonder if you are, Uncle. Let me read my letter first. This is my father speaking to me."

Johann then sat down opposite his uncle, and for ten minutes there was silence in the room except for the rustle of paper. When he had finished, Hans noticed that his eyes were bright with excitement. Surely it was excitement and not grief?

"Well, my boy? Are you going to show me the letter? I should like to read what my only brother has said to my only nephew."

Johann got up and tossed the letter into his uncle's lap.

"Go on, then. Read it. You know enough English, don't you? He's written all this in English. He trusted me, you see. He knew I'd learn English. I don't agree with all he says, but I shall go to this place in England he talks about . . . Go on. Read it."

Hans Schmidt took the closely-written sheets, settled his spectacles on his nose, and read – more slowly than Johann because his knowledge of English was not so good.

NOT SCARLET BUT GOLD

My dear Son,

You cannot remember me and will only read these words because I am dead. Your dear mother who will give you this on your 18th birthday does not know what I am saying to you, but you will be wise to let her read these words because what I have to say concerns her too. I am writing this in English because it is my wish that you should learn to speak and write this language as well as I can do, and because, whatever the outcome of this unhappy war, I am convinced that English is the most important language in the world.

I am writing this because I may never return from my next duty for my Fatherland and because I believe that Germany cannot win this war. I, like you, my son, am a German, and until recently I have been proud of our country and its struggles to be worthy of our great men whose names enrich history. I hate this war but have never hated the British, but it is my duty to fight for my country. Better men than I are dying for it, and even death for us of this generation may be worthwhile if you – now only a baby – and your generation may live in peace without the threat of war.

I write this a few hours before being dropped with some other comrades by parachute over Britain. If I am successful in my mission and am lucky, I shall be picked up within three or four weeks and brought back to Germany where I shall see you and your mother again. When I land in England I shall think, behave and speak like an Englishman, for on that my life depends. It is because I am qualified by experience and study to do this that I am being sent. As you read this letter, you will know that I have failed, because if I do not return, this letter will be delivered to your mother by a comrade I can trust because he thinks as I do. You, who never knew me, however, can be sure that I shall do my duty if possible, although I detest what I have to do. I am a saboteur, *and it is my job to get inside some of the big factories round Birmingham, in the English Midlands, to stir up discontent and to bribe the grumblers and try to make them strike and generally cause trouble. I shall be provided with forged papers, with certain tools and weapons, with food, English money in notes and with radio. Four of us are to be dropped in wild, lonely hill country in the county of Shropshire, which you will find easily enough on a map of England. These hills are called the Long Mynd and the Stiperstones and I hope you will see them under very different conditions one day. When you go, you will remember how your father was dropped there one black night – one of four others against millions of the enemy. Our job – and we shall work separately – will be to hide ourselves in those hills until we can find the best way of reaching the Midland cities. It is probable that some of us will fail, and even if we all succeed I am still certain that Germany can never win this war because the world is against her.*

Somewhere then in these hills called Stiperstones or Long Mynd, you, my son, may find considerable sums of British banknotes. Until we land, we shall not know where to hide what we bring, for we shall not be able to carry on our persons all the money. We may find friendly agents living near by, but we are told that this country is wild, lonely and haunted so that the locals fear it. There are old mines there and it will be out duty to establish hidden bases from which to work – but where these will be I cannot say.

I write these words only an hour before leaving Germany and because you read them now it is probable that I have failed my country. If you are able to go to England and search for the money, you must imagine yourself to be a spy in enemy country, but you must be as English in speech and appearance as the English. I cannot tell how you will be received years after I write these words. You may have no need to go. You may not wish to go, but I believe there will be a good chance of your finding money that I risked my life to carry – but you will have to be as clever to find it as I was to hide it.

Share this letter with your mother now that you have read it and may you make a wise decision.

God bless you, my son.
Your affectionate
Father.

Hans sat silent for a long minute as he put down the last sheet of this remarkable letter. He was remembering his brother as he had last seen him when he was on leave a few days before this had been written. Those who were close to him had guessed that he was on some secret war work, but not his fears nor his obvious hatred of war against the British. Nobody now would ever know how or when or where he died. "On active service" was all that his wife had been told.

"How can you sit there and say nothing?" Johann blazed suddenly at his uncle. "You'll have to find enough money to get me to England. That's the least you can do. I'm going to find those hidden banknotes. I need the money badly. I'm in a bit of trouble, but if you help me over this I can soon fix everything. I know a way of getting a British passport if there's any trouble. You'll have to help me, Uncle Hans."

The older man passed Johann the letter.

"Just remember that this letter was written in the stress and strain of war. Your father was a very brave man, Johann, but we know nothing of his death, nor if he was captured first, not if he was successful in hiding this English money. Even if he did so, we do not know whether it was found by others, nor have we any clue as to where he hid it."

"Of course we haven't! I'm going to look for one. I'll explore every inch of that country. You've got to find the money for me to go."

"No, Johann. I'll have no hand in this. You say you're in trouble now. What have you done? Are the police looking for you? Why don't you tell me the truth? Where are you living and what are you doing?"

"I'm going to live my own life my own way. You wouldn't understand if I told you. You're too old."

"But not too old to give you money, Johann."

"You'll get it all back when I find my father's money. Can't you see that I've *got* to go to England just as soon as I can. He wanted me to have it and I'm going to find it. I shall go as an Englishman – not a German. Are you going to lend me enough to get me over there? Make up your mind, because if you won't I shall get it somewhere else. I wish I hadn't been soft and shown you the letter . . . I'm not staying here tonight, but I'll come back in the morning. If you won't help me then, you'll regret it. Think it over, Uncle. You've disappointed me."

Before Hans Schmidt could answer, Johann slammed the door of the flat behind him and the older man was left alone with his thoughts.

CHAPTER 2

The Handsome Hiker

On a blustery morning in the Easter holidays, a week or so after the events described in the last chapter, Petronella Sterling was riding alone on her Welsh pony Sally across the top of the Long Mynd.

She loved this country more than any place she had ever known. She loved the solitude of the hills, the sound of the wind and the sight of the billowy clouds all throwing racing shadows across the stony slopes of the mountain called the Stiperstones some four or five miles ahead.

She watched a shadow almost like an enormous black curtain come sliding silently towards her, and suddenly the sun had gone and the wind was cold enough for her to fasten the warm collar of her jacket. She turned Sally and looked back the way she had come, watching the shadow pass and the sun light up the Stretton hills to the east.

Sally turned her head as if sympathising with her mistress's mood, and Peter patted her neck and blinked away a tear.

"I can't believe it, Sally. I still can't believe that we've got to leave here for good. And I don't know what's going to happen to *you* when we go to live in Hereford with Uncle Micah. I hadn't the courage to ask Daddy just now because I know how he hated telling me that we've got to leave Hatchholt . . . He's getting old, Sally. When he was telling me all this at breakfast I could see suddenly that it wasn't right for him to be alone there so much . . . And now I'm nearly sorry that we're going to Seven Gates today. I'm not so sure that I want to go. Perhaps I'm getting old too?"

She slipped off the pony's back, sat down facing the sun, took a letter from the pocket of her jeans and re-read it for the fifth time since she had received it three days ago:

Post Office,
Barton Beach.

Dear Peter,

I've got wonderful news but perhaps you know it already. I hope you do but if you don't this is it and it's funny because Mary has written to me and asks me to tell you in case David hasn't written but of course he writes to you regularly so I expect you know. Everything is fixed up now for us to meet at Seven Gates on Monday.

David and the twins are coming by train and they are bringing this new girl called Harriet Sparrow because she's got to be made a member of the Club now. I expect this girl is very nice but I think we've got enough members of this Club. Anyway Peter I've got lots of romantic things to tell you and it's wonderful to think I won't be lonely any more like I am in term time so please come over to Seven Gates soon as you can on Monday. I expect I'll be there first because I'm nearest but if you come really early will you call for me at home? But perhaps I'd better be first there so I can help to get everything ready. Mary says they're bringing some food as their share of the camp but now I've written all this and not said a word about Tom. I hope he's coming too but he's always so busy on the farm and he doesn't know how I absolutely pine *for him. I've written to him too but I don't suppose I'll get an answer. I've got so much to tell you I can hardly wait so roll on Monday is what I say.*

Your loving friend
Jenny.

From the moment she had first befriended the lonely but romantic Jenny, Peter had laughed at the way Jenny expressed herself. She was just as breathless when she spoke and hadn't much use for full stops, but she was going to be thrilled when Peter gave her the letter from Tom Ingles which he had brought over to Hatchholt.

Peter hugged her knees as she looked across to the outline of the rock-crowned hill called Caer Caradoc on the other side of Stretton vale. There was plenty of time, for she wasn't yet sure when she wanted to arrive at her cousin's farm called Seven Gates, and she wanted to sort things out for herself. She was indeed feeling more unhappy and hurt than at any other time since she first went away to school.

Peter could not remember her mother who had died when she was a baby, and her companionship with her father was rare. She had known for some years how wise he had been to send her away to school and how much he had wanted her to find friends of her own age. And it had turned out that one of the most important days of her life had been when David Morton and the twins, Dickie and Mary, had come for the first time to the old farmhouse called Witchend. Apart from a few girls at school, the Mortons, Jenny and Tom and the cousins Jon and Penny Warrender, who lived far to the south in Sussex, became Peter's only friends through the Lone Pine Club that David and she had founded soon after their first meeting. Most holidays the Mortons came to stay for a while in the old farmhouse. They had shared many adventures together in these hills and Peter knew for certain this morning that they had been the happiest times of her life. And this next week might well be the last holiday of its sort, because she and her father were now to leave the only home she had ever known, to live on the outskirts of Hereford with her father's brother Uncle Micah, who had once owned Seven Gates which was now farmed by his son

Charles. No doubt she would often be invited to stay at Seven Gates and when Mr and Mrs Morton were at Witchend she might be asked to stay with them, but something had gone wrong there too.

David was the trouble. For a long time now Peter had known that when she was a little older she was not going to be interested in any other man more than David Morton. He didn't say much, but she knew that she had become important to him too. She liked writing letters, but he loathed it and something had gone wrong this term. They had not met at Christmas but had exchanged presents. She had sent him a wallet and taken nearly an hour in three shops to choose it, in Shrewsbury, one Saturday afternoon. He had sent her a book which had delighted her but had never written to thank her. The twins had thanked her for their presents but had only mentioned David casually, and then she had been very stupid and decided not to write to him again until he had written to her. But no letter had come and, what was even worse, he had written to Jenny giving her a message to pass on – just as if Peter was a casual acquaintance rather than the best friend he was ever likely to have!

Then suddenly her face flamed at the thought which had never occurred to her before. Perhaps he had never received the wallet and was wondering why she hadn't remembered him at Christmas? But, of course, he wasn't like that. Surely she knew him better? He'd just got sick of the whole business and was extra busy with exams at school and having a wonderful social time in London over the holidays. If that was so, why should the Mortons suddenly decide to come to Seven Gates and not to Witchend? The answer to that question was probably that when their parents did not come up to Shropshire they all preferred to camp in the old barn at Seven Gates which Charles Sterling allowed the Lone

Piners to use. This barn was only across the farmyard and Charles' young wife Trudie kept a watchful eye on the twins and enjoyed doing so. Anyway, they all loved Trudie, and Peter had always admired her cousin Charles.

Then Sally camp up and nuzzled at her pocket for sugar. Peter gave the pony two lumps, swung into the saddle and urged her into a trot as another mass of cloud filled the western sky. There was something odd and suddenly forbidding about these clouds and once, above the sound of Sally's drumming hooves, Peter thought she heard the distant rumble of thunder.

Ahead of her now, stretching like a grey silk ribbon to her right and left, was the Portway – one of the loneliest and oldest roads in Britain.

Peter crossed the Portway and took a narrow stony track leading up to the highest point of the Mynd, where she stopped and looked down on the patchwork of fields below her. Then she looked up at the Stiperstones ahead, expecting to see on the summit the curious formation of rocks called the Devil's Chair. With a sudden shock she realised that it wasn't there. The jagged spine along the highest ridge had vanished too, in the clouds now shrouding the top of the mountain.

Peter, who was not really superstitious, was shocked because she knew that many who lived round the Stiperstones said, even these days, that when it was no longer possible to see the Devil's Chair, then the devil himself was sitting on his throne and that trouble was on the way.

"Come on, Sally," she said quietly. "Down we go and let's not worry about the old devil. The clouds may move soon, but there's a big storm coming."

Sally, sure-footed and unperturbed about devils on their thrones, started down the steep track, while Peter's thoughts went back to winter evenings in the

THE HANDSOME HIKER

tiny kitchen at Hatchholt when the fire gleamed red behind the bars of the grate and her father told her legends of Shropshire.

Even though the sun came out again so that she could see the Devil's Chair ahead as she rode, Peter was not in the mood to dismiss all the old stories as nonsense. More than once the Lone Piners had been sure that they had broken the spell of the Stiperstones, but they had been in real danger each time: and once she had broken her ankle in a cave in which they had been trapped. Seven Gates was a happier, brighter place now that it belonged to her cousins Charles and Trudie, and the Lone Piners were always welcome there: but David seemed to have arranged this particular holiday and she was unhappy about him. Once again she was in half a mind to turn back to Hatchholt, but then she remembered that her father was going to Hereford to discuss future plans with Uncle Micah. She had to go through with this. Perhaps they would have fun: and it would be great to see the twins again and their new friend Harriet Sparrow. Perhaps after all they would be happier than ever before at Seven Gates, and everything might be so wonderful between her and David that she would be able to forget the misery of leaving Hatchholt and the realisation that her father was getting old. It would be great to share all her worries with David as she had always done.

Peter was within a mile of the narrow road which ran under the flank of the mountain when she realised that the uncertain weather was changing for the worse. The Devil's Chair had vanished again in the mists, and the sky to the west was thick and lowering with dark clouds. A mutter of thunder in the distance unsettled the pony, who hated it, and Peter had no difficulty in encouraging her to canter. They reached the road before the next crash came and then, as Peter soothed Sally, the storm broke and the road was white with bouncing hailstones which stung her face and her hands.

Suddenly she remembered that just off the road near here was a ruined cottage where she could shelter, so she urged Sally forward, trying, as she did so, to shield her face from the stinging hail.

Then the hail turned to rain and, through the grey curtain, Peter saw on her right the shape of the cottage and an outbuilding standing back from the road. There was no gate now, but Peter forced Sally through a gap in the wall towards a ruined stable.

Thankfully she slipped from Sally's back and led her into shelter. There was not much roof left, but the far corner under the manger was reasonably dry, and there Peter made a fuss of the pony and quietened her down. Then she realised that there was not enough dry room for both of them in the stable. The rain was still heavy and she could see the water gushing from the broken gutters of the cottage and pouring down its stone walls. There was no glass in the windows and the place looked grim and forbidding. Only at the back had the slates slipped from the rotting rafters so she decided to shelter just inside the front of the cottage.

With a reassuring word to Sally she dashed out of the stable, through the forest of weeds and into the doorway which led straight into a stone-flagged room. Although dry, this was a horrid room. Tatters of discoloured paper hung from the walls, the old fireplace was rusty and full of rubbish, while in one corner the ceiling had collapsed leaving a pile of messy plaster on the floor. In the other corner a door, hanging on one hinge, led into a back room.

Peter took off her jacket and shook it, and then looked ruefully at her soaked jeans. They were very uncomfortable, but she had just decided that they might as well dry on her when suddenly she heard, above the roar of the rain, the crunch of a step behind her. She stifled a scream which rose in her throat and then, with a hand to her mouth, she found the courage to turn round.

In the doorway was standing the most handsome young man she had ever seen. For what seemed a long minute they stared at each other. Peter, with her back to the window, could see him clearly and she never quite forgot her first sight of him. His face was tanned, his dark hair was wet and untidy like her own, and his eyes grey and strangely compelling. This was no ghost and her heart thumped as he smiled, showing very white and even teeth.

"I'm sorry," he said. "I scared you. I came in here to shelter. Same as you, I suppose, but you're wetter than I am. Got far to go?"

His voice was as attractive as his looks and Peter, to her annoyance, found herself blushing. She felt suddenly shy and ran her fingers through her hair, thinking what a sight she must look. Then, just because his approving look made her shyer still, she began to chatter in a way unnatural to her. "Yes, you did scare me. I never though of anyone else being here, particularly as this place is haunted. I must have surprised you too, but I promise I'm not a ghost."

"No," he smiled. "I can see that. How do you know that this old ruin is haunted?"

"Everyone around here says so. A witch used to live in it. Do you believe in witches? I've got a friend who does. She lives over the other side of the mountain."

He leaned back against the doorpost.

"Do you live round here yourself then? It's wonderful country and I'm trying to explore it on a walking holiday. I've never been here before. I like it."

"I'm glad you do. I think it's wonderful, but then you see I've lived in these hills practically all my life – except when I'm at school, of course."

"Surely you're not still at school? You look the sort of girl who ought to have finished with school by now."

Peter blushed again, realising that she was rather pleased that she didn't look like a schoolgirl. He was certainly very charming as well as good-looking.

"I'm not going to school much longer. I live about eight miles away and I'm on my way to join some friends at a farm called Seven Gates quite near here. I've got a pony who is scared of thunderstorms out there in the old stable. . . . And that reminds me, if it's stopped raining I must be on my way."

"Don't go yet," he said. "Tell me who you are. You're much too nice to run away as soon as we're beginning to know each other."

Peter looked at him in surprise as he moved away from the doorway towards her. She wasn't used to this sort of remark, and although she felt that she ought to protest, she was secretly rather flattered because he wasn't treating her like a child. She fidgeted with her hair again and turned towards the door.

"Please don't be silly," she begged. "Of course I must go. My cousins at Seven Gates are expecting me."

He followed her out into the wilderness of a garden. It had stopped raining and the sun was shining again, although water was still tinkling in the gutters. Peter looked up at the mountain and saw the Devil's Chair clear against the skyline. Suddenly everything seemed to be brighter and she turned and smiled at him. It was nice to be admired and she could see the appraisal in his eyes.

"You needn't hurry for a few minutes. I've had a long wait and I was feeling lonely when you turned up. What's your name? Rose? If your parents called you Rose, they chose well."

"You really are absurd. My name is Petronella

THE HANDSOME HIKER

Sterling and I live with my father in a cottage on the other side of the Long Mynd . . . My friends call me Peter, which is rather silly really. What's *your* name and where do you come from"

"I'd like to call you Peter, but I must say that to call a girl like you by a boy's name doesn't make much sense . . . Are you going to this farm for a holiday? I'd like to meet you again and ask you to help me explore this country. I'm interested in it."

"But why? What do you want to know? And who are you and why do you keep asking these questions?"

He looked at her so meaningly that her heart began to thump again and she ran over to the old stable before he could answer. He followed her, and as she led Sally out into the watery sunshine he put a hand on the horse's bridle.

"Nice pony," he said. "Are you going to meet me again, Peter? I want a friendly guide to show me the Long Mynd and the Stiperstones, and if you've lived here all your life you're just the girl for me. Shall we meet tomorrow?"

Peter struggled into her rucksack and swung herself on to Sally's back.

"You're talking nonsense," she said. "Of course I'm not going to meet you tomorrow or any other day. And anyway, you haven't told me who you are or why you're so anxious to explore these hills . . Please take your hand off Sally's bridle."

He smiled again but did not move his hand.

"My name," he said, "is John Smith. Just that. Plain John Smith. I live in Birmingham and am at the University. I'm reading geography and I'm writing a history of this district. I've read a lot about it and now I'm trying to explore it, but even with a map it's not very easy. I want someone like you to show me round.

Someone who has always lived here and knows everybody who lives in these hills. Why don't you help me, Peter? We'd have a lot of fun, I promise you."

She looked down into his bold eyes and was inclined to believe him! Then she pulled herself together. Somehow he didn't look like a Midlander and neither did he speak like one.

"You're being absurd," she said. "Let me go, please. I must go and meet my friends."

He stepped back.

"Very well, Peter. I shall come and see you at this farm called Seven Gates. We shall meet again, you can be sure."

As she rode Sally out into the road she saw a rainbow over the Stiperstones. She was tempted to look back once and was not surprised to see John Smith smiling at her and raising his hand in salutation.

CHAPTER 3

Seven Gates

About the time that Peter was sheltering in the ruined cottage, her friend Jenny Harman was on her way from her home in Barton Beach to Seven Gates. As she cycled up the hill to the first of the white gates after which the farm was named, the storm broke.

Jenny was a redhead with snub nose and freckles. She hated cycling and hated thunderstorms and, although she was excited at the prospect of meeting her friends and camping out in the old barn, she felt a particular grudge against the weather. The hail stung her face, the back wheel skidded and the knapsack on her back suddenly seemed to weigh a ton. As she reached the gate she thankfully jumped off her bike, left it where it fell and crawled for shelter under the wooden platform on which the farmer left his milk churns for collection. It was uncomfortable but better than getting wet through.

The road was white with hailstones, thunder was rumbling round the Stiperstones, and this seemed to Jenny a very poor beginning to a holiday. She had the sudden feeling that something unpleasant was going to happen and wished that they were all going to Witchend, where she would certainly have a chance of seeing Tom. She remembered the evening when she had first met Peter, almost at this very place, and had been scared to go up through the wood with her to the house. Seven Gates was a very different house now and had been painted so that it was bright and cheerful – and everybody liked Peter's cousin Charles and his pretty young wife Trudie. Although Jenny now got on very much better with her stepmother, Barton Beach was a gloomy village, not much fun, and the holidays were often boring when she didn't see Tom or Peter or the other Lone Piners.

Then the hail turned to rain, and a few minutes later the sun was shining. Jenny crawled out of her shelter, picked up her bike and pushed it up the track, through two more white gates into the farmyard. The slate roof of the farmhouse was steaming in the sunshine and as Jenny splashed through the puddles in the yard she looked with pleasurable anticipation at the white doors (the seventh gate) of the big barn opposite the house, which was the second headquarters of the Lone Pine Club.

Trudie Sterling had seen her from the kitchen window and opened the door.

"Hullo, Jenny. You're the first. I'm pleased to see you because I'm feeling lonely. Charles has gone to Craven Arms in the car to meet the others. How are you? You're looking weather-beaten but nice."

"Oh, thank you, Trudie. It's wonderful to be here again, and if you'll give me the key of the barn I'll open it up and perhaps I ought to light the stove and try and get the place ready. How are you, Trudie? It's very kind of you to have us here."

Trudie said, "Come inside and have a hot rock cake. I've been baking some for you all and may as well try one out on you . . . And take off your anorak and leave it here to dry."

So Jenny sat on the kitchen table and swung her legs and puffed out steam as she bit into a bun.

"How's Tom?" Trudie asked. "Neglecting you as usual?"

Jenny didn't really mind being teased by wasn't quite sure whether this remark was teasing or not.

"I hope Peter's got a message for me. Tom will come if he can, I know . . . Do you think I ought to tell him that I pine for him, Trudie?"

"Never, never, never, Jenny. Not until you're married to him anyhow . . . Now go and sweep out the barn. The others will be here in about an hour if the train's on time. . . . Here's the key."

"And here's Peter," Jenny called from the open door as Peter rode into the farmyard. "Hullo, Peter! I've only just arrived and we've only got an hour before the others come . . . Were you caught in the storm? Isn't this fun? You look excited."

Peter slid off the pony's back and struggled out of her heavy knapsack before she answered.

"I had to shelter in the witch's cottage. Take my baggage into the barn, Jenny, while I look after Sally . . . And what do you mean about me looking excited?"

Before Jenny could answer, Trudie came out and gave Peter, who had been her bridesmaid, an affectionate hug.

"Nice to see you again, darling. We don't see enough of you here. How's your father?"

"Come over to the stable, Trudie. I want to tell you something. Please open up the barn, Jenny. I won't be long."

Jenny shrugged but did as she was asked. She was sure that Peter was excited about something but had little doubt that she would soon find out all she wanted to know.

Meanwhile, in the stable, Peter looking straight at Trudie over Sally's head, said, "Daddy has just told me that we've got to leave Hatchholt and go and live with Uncle Micah and Aunt Carol near Hereford. This is about the most terrible thing that has ever happened to me, Trudie. Did you know?"

"We were sure it would have to happen soon, Peter, and Charles said only the other day that it will be up to you to make it as easy as you can for your father. He won't like leaving Hatchholt any more than you do . . There always have to be changes, Peter. You're growing up and soon leaving school, and it's best for your father and Charles' father to be together now, so don't look so tragic. You're always welcome here in the holidays and no doubt you'll go to Witchend whenever the Mortons come up."

Peter felt her eyes filling with tears.

"I'm a fool to be so upset, of course, but I was sure you'd understand how I feel, Trudie. I suppose you and Charles have been talking about me and feeling sorry for me. I don't like people feeling sorry for me."

This outburst was so unlike Peter that Trudie was surprised.

"Anything else upset you, Peter? I'm not particularly sorry for you about Hatchholt. Your father couldn't go on living there for ever and I don't suppose you would always be there either . . . Anyway, go and help Jenny now. I'll rub Sally down and we'll both have a talk with Charles about this soon."

Peter, looking a little ashamed, gave her half a smile.

"Oh, I know you're right, Trudie, but this has all been rather sudden. Don't tell the others, please. I don't want them to know yet. Will you swear?"

"I swear. And don't fret, Peter. Have a good time this week and forget your troubles."

So Peter, who could trust Trudie to look after Sally, ran over to the barn which Jenny had now opened up. The barn was a remarkable building. It was vaulted and pillared like a church and the uneven floor was of brick. Along the left-hand wall there were several big wooden partitions, once used for storage but now used by the boys as a dormitory. The girls slept in a granary upstairs. In the far right-hand corner was an old iron cookingstove which the Lone Piners used on special occasions. Tonight, when the others arrived, would be such an occasion, for they always celebrated their reunions with a feast.

As Peter stood in the doorway, still feeling rather unhappy, Jenny, with a broom, advanced towards her behind a cloud of dust.

"Oh, Peter," she spluttered. "We shall never get the place looking nice if you don't come and help . . And I do wish you'd cheer up, I've been saving up so many exciting things to talk to you about . . . And that reminds me, Peter. Have you got a letter for me . . . From Tom, I mean . . . And you did get one from me, didn't you?"

Peter backed away from the dust-storm, grabbed Jenny's broom and pulled her out into the sunshine.

"It's much better to leave the dust to settle, Jen. When we can see our way round, we'll put up the trestle-table, get out the crockery, start the fire and put a kettle on the stove. But don't let's spend the time sweeping."

Jenny sneezed violently. "Peter. HAVE YOU GOT A LETTER FOR ME?"

"Yes. I have. Here it is, and thank you for yours. Tom's all right and he'll maybe visit in a day or two."

Jenny snatched her letter and leaned against the door-post to read it while Peter went back to the barn and got out the trestles for the table. When Jenny came back, she said, "Tom doesn't often write to me, Peter. It's rather wonderful when he does, although he never seems to say anything really *personal* . . . He says he'll come when he can, but Uncle Alf Ingles is rather keen on work just at present . . You know something, Peter? Tom thinks the club is kids' stuff. I don't care what people say because it's so wonderful for me to have a chance to see you all. What do you and David think about the club? Do you think it's stupid?"

Peter, who was lifting crockery out of an old trunk, had her back to Jenny when she answered.

"I don't know, Jenny. The twins still like it and Harriet wants to join. I don't know what David thinks. It doesn't really matter though, does it? These cups are filthy. Nip over to the kitchen and get a bucket of water and we'll wash them before the others arrive."

Although Jenny was a chatterbox she was very shrewd. She was very fond of Peter and was aware that something had upset her. Other people's happiness meant a lot to the romantic Jenny. She hated the idea of quarrelling between her friends and determined to find out what was wrong. It would be disastrous for them all if Peter and David were unhappy at the beginning of their holiday.

Jenny couldn't be subtle however hard she tried, and so, as they worked together cleaning and tidying and putting up the table, she spoke out just exactly what was in her mind.

"I suppose you know that David wrote to me and asked me to cycle over to Witchend and get the old tin with our oath in it from under the pine tree? He wants it so that this new girl Harriet can sign her name in blood just like we all did when we were made members. I've got the tin safe in my knapsack, and if David asked me to fetch it he can't be too fed up with the club, can he? . . . Why, Peter, what's the matter? Have I said something awful?"

"Did David say *why* he wanted you to go to Witchend, Jenny? I haven't heard from him for ages and it would have been easier to *me* to go."

"Peter! Is everything *all right* between you and David? I can keep a secret if you'd like to tell me about it."

Peter shook her head miserably.

"Nothing to tell, Jenny. I suppose we've both been too busy to write. David is like Tom – hates letters: and that's why I wondered why he'd written to you."

"It wasn't anything special, Peter. I expect he thought

I'd got more time than you because I'm not away at school. And I expect he thought I'd go over to Ingles when Tom was so near and so I did, of course. That's why he wrote to *me*."

"Of course that's why," Peter said, a shade too brightly. "Don't you worry about us, Jenny. Let's go up to our attic and tidy that up. We shall have Harriet and Mary tonight. You'll like Harriet. She's fun and she's been longing to come up here and meet you."

The girls always stuffed hay into sacks and used these as mattresses under their sleeping-bags, and Charles had thoughtfully left four bales up in the granary for them. Jenny, chattering away nineteen to the dozen, suddenly said, "Peter. Would you like to tell me what's wrong? Is it just David?"

Peter knew then how lucky she was to have such good friends. Jenny really was fantastic and as she looked at her eager little freckled face Peter was sure that she could tell her about her father, and moving from Hatchholt, and that she had the feeling that their meetings were never going to be the same again. Jenny would understand. But even as she opened her mouth to speak, the chance had gone, for through the window she saw Charles' Land-Rover drive into the farmyard.

"They're here!" Jenny shouted. "Come on down and meet them, Peter."

But Peter, suddenly scared of meeting David, stayed where she was, kneeling on her sleeping-bag and watching through the window. The Land-Rover was laden with luggage. Charles got out first and kissed his wife who was there to greet them, and then let down the tailboard. Out tumbled the twins and their Scottie dog Macbeth, followed by Harriet Sparrow looking shy and bewildered.

As the granary window had not been made to open, Peter could not hear what anybody was saying, but the twins seemed to be shouting or singing as they danced round Trudie, and Mackie was certainly barking with excitement. Then David got out and, after greeting Trudie, turned round quickly as Jenny ran across the farmyard.

Peter's heart thumped as she watched him. Was it imagination or did he really look older? He smiled at Jenny and Peter realized that she would make a fool of herself if she didn't go down at once. It would never do for David to get the idea that she was afraid to meet him.

The meeting wasn't so difficult after all because the twins rushed at her as she ran across the floor of the barn.

"Petah, you beast," Mary said as she hugged her. "You weren't here to meet us! Ever since London we've been talking about you and hoping you'd come to the station."

"I didn't hope *that*," Dickie grinned. "I'm hungry. What I want tonight is a prodigious banquet and what I hoped was that you'd remember we'd be famishin' and start cooking things. Is anything cooking, Peter?"

"Not yet, Dickie. Who told you about prodigious banquets? Is prodigious your latest word?"

"Yes, it is, and it's a good word. I read it somewhere. They have dancing girls at feasts, I hope, and Harriet is going to be the dancing girl. All new members have to do something like that, don't they?"

Then Harriet Sparrow came into the barn. Her pale face was flushed and her eyes bright with excitement. She had already shared two adventures with the Lone Piners and had become firm friends with those she had met and for long had been looking forward to coming to Shropshire. She had not met Jenny before, and the others, greeting her in the yard, seemed to have forgotten that. Harriet was shy and Jenny was a little jealous of her, so they'd looked quickly at each other and left it at that. Then Harriet heard the twins chattering to Peter and made her escape from an awkward moment.

"Peter, this is wonderful! I never guessed that Seven Gates was like this. It's far, far more mysterious than you said. I haven't *really* got to be a dancing girl, have I? I heard what Dickie said, but I don't believe him."

They were still laughing when David strolled in and said casually, "Hullo Pete. Good to see you again. What have you been doing with yourself all this time?"

She couldn't see him clearly because he had his back to the light, but his voice didn't sound quite natural. He was nervous too and it was silly of him to ask what she'd been doing with herself when he'd never written.

So all she said was, "Hullo, David. You all seem in fine form and it's good to see Harriet. Tom's coming in a day or two if he can, but I expect Jenny's told you that already." Then she added, "I hope your parents are well?"

At once she was aware that she too had said the wrong thing. For years now Mrs Morton had treated her almost as a daughter and whenever they met she had been quietly accepted as part of the Morton family. And now, in a stiff and silly way she had referred to these two loved people as "your parents".

She flushed and looked down at the twins, who were staring at her in amazement. David glanced away and Mary said, "Mummy and Daddy are fine Petah. They sent their love. Let's unpack and get busy. I'm like Dickie. My appetite is prodigious."

They worked for the next hour and a half. Knapsacks were unpacked, sleeping-bags unrolled. David and Dickie fetched fuel and lit the stove, which promptly filled the barn with smoke. Harriet was shown the granary where she was to sleep, and then the banquet was prepared. Peter took Harriet over to the farm kitchen so that she could get to know Trudie, and there they peeled potatoes. Presently Jenny wandered over and patronised Harriet a little because she couldn't possibly know anything about camping out or living like this in the country and, more than anything else perhaps, because she was a new girl.

"Mary and I are ready to start cooking as soon as the stove is going," Jenny suggested. "The only thing we could cook now is smoked haddock or kippers. David says there must be a bird's nest in the chimney. I hope you're not nervous of ghosts and things like that, Harriet. Did you know those hills round here are haunted? Most peculiar things happen. Omens happen. When we have time we'll tell you about the Devil's Chair."

"Don't be silly, Jenny," Peter said. "We've told Harriet all the old stories. Go and find Trudie and ask if we can borrow her enormous frying-pan again."

"OK," Jenny agreed cheerfully. "All the same, Harriet ought to be warned. I don't want to be wakened up in the night by her if she gets scared. And another thing, Peter. I didn't have time before the others came to tell you about the most exciting and romantic thing that happened to me yesterday. Remind me presently and I'll tell you all at the prodigious banquet."

Peter laughed. "You won't need reminding, Jenny. Nothing will *stop* you telling us."

It was nearly dark when the three girls walked back to the barn. The stove was now roaring cheerfully and David was lighting the hurricane lamps hanging from the great oak beams. Mary had laid the table and her twin was sticking candles into the necks of empty bottles. They always ate by candlelight after dark, although Charles Sterling made a firm rule that no naked lights were allowed when they went to bed.

"Someone might cut up a loaf," Peter suggested as she put the frying-pan on the stove. "Jenny and I will do the cooking tonight," and after that there seemed no particular reason to say anything special to David.

"Shut the doors now. Shut the doors," Dickie shouted as the fat began to frizzle in the pan. "Let's have a lovely fug. Are you feeling nervous, Harry? Have you practised your dance? I bet you wish you hadn't come with us. I bet you wish you hadn't to go through with what you've got to go through with, if you know what I mean."

So Mary led Harriet out into the farmyard and closed the great white doors behind them. "Do you see what we mean about Seven Gates now, Harry? Isn't it wonderful? I'm sure there's not another place like this in all the world. Witchend is marvellous, of course, and we'll never stop going there. Witchend is sort of romantic, but Seven Gates is thrilling and exciting and mysterious."

It was dark now and the stars seemed to be moving as the clouds scurried across the night sky. Two of the windows in the house were aglow and they looked like the lights of a happy home. Below them the wind stirred the treetops of the whispering wood, and away to their right behind the barn loomed the great shape of the mountain.

"So that's the Stiperstone up there, Mary. When will you take me to see it? Can we climb to the top?"

"Of course we can. It's not so bad in daylight, but it's true, Harry, that the sun doesn't often shine up there. Often there's a mist and it rains a lot. Jenny said there was a terrible thunderstorm this afternoon and Peter got wet through riding over on Sally. I pretend I'm not really afraid, but it's a ghostly place all the same. Peculiar things do happen round here."

"Mary, I haven't *really* got to be a dancing girl, have I? You wouldn't make me do anything like that? Really and truly I'm a member of the Club already and this is only the ceremony, isn't it?"

Mary laughed. "That's all. You have to sign what

Dickie calls the dokkerment in your own blood, but that isn't too bad. I'll help you. Come on. Let's go back now."

They flung back the doors of the barn and were met by a blast of hot air and the blue smoke of frying. The table was laid and the candles in the bottles were alight. Jenny and Peter with damp, scarlet faces were still busy over the stove and Dickie was getting in the way. David, Jenny noticed with misgiving, was leaning against one of the partitions with his hands in his pockets and not looking too cheerful. She did her best to get things going.

"We'd better eat before everything bursts into flames, and I hope it tastes better than it smells," she said. "You've got to sit at the top of the table, David, because you're the captain. Peter must sit next to you and I've promised to look after the victim."

"She's got to be a dancing girl," Dickie protested. "There's always dancing girls at feasts. She's got to be blindfolded and I think she ought to be led up to the Devil's Chair in the dark where all the witches are flying round on their broomsticks. It's all wrong to make it easy for Harry, although we do like her very much."

"The only thing that will keep Dickie quiet is food," Jenny laughed. "Come on, David. Hold the plates for us instead of lazing over there and we'll fill them up. Peter and I have done our share of the work this evening and you others will have to wash up."

Five minutes later there was comparative silence, for even the twins found eating more important than talking. Once or twice Jenny looked across the flickering candles to David and Peter, but they didn't seem to have anything to say to each other, and she was now sure that she had never seen the latter so preoccupied. Although they all knew Peter to be rather reserved, she had never been secretive to her friends. There was no doubt now that she really had something on her mind, and Jenny determined that before they went to sleep tonight she would find out what it was. Surely it had something to do with David?

Then Dickie, with a sigh of satisfaction, looked searchingly at his empty plate and then across at Jenny. He winked and then glanced at Harriet.

"You're slow, Harry. Better make the best of this meal before we get out the dokkerment which I suppose somebody has forgotten to bring."

"No, they haven't," David said briskly. "Jenny remembered. She's been over to get it and she gave it to me just now. Here it is," and from his pocket he produced the rusty old tin which was kept buried in the soil at the foot of the solitary pine tree on the hillside above Witchend. He opened it and brought out the folded paper – Dickie's "dokkerment"! The ink was faded now and the members' signatures in their own blood were almost unreadable. How long ago and rather childish the founding of this secret club seemed! And yet perhaps there was still something in it? David looked up to see Peter watching him and wondered what she was thinking.

"Are you wondering whether some of us are getting too old for the Lone Pine Club, David?" she said quietly. "Don't worry too much about that, but read out the rules so that Harry knows what she's doing. Maybe it won't hurt some of us to hear them again ... Go on, David. You're still the captain. Tell Harry what she's joining: then she'll sign."

David flushed and, as he unfolded the paper, he realised that they were all sitting there in silence. The twins were looking at Peter in surprise, Harriet was looking down at her hands clasped tight in her lap and Jenny was staring unhappily at him. There was a sudden atmosphere of tension which was broken by Mary.

"Harry knows all about the Club. She's had two big adventures with us and she belongs. We want her in and she's really a member already, but we had to wait for the signing until we could bring her up here."

"All right, Mary," David said. "I realise Harry knows all about us and I've only one suggestion to make before the ceremony. With Tom and Jon and Penny who aren't here we've got eight members. Harriet makes nine. That's enough. I propose we stick at nine. There's no sense in getting any bigger. All agreed?"

"Oh, dear!" Harriet whispered. "You make it sound as if you don't really want me, David."

"Don't you start being silly too, Harry," Peter said quite sharply. "Of course we want you. David isn't being very tactful, but I know he means that nine friends who promise to stick together are enough. By the rules none of us can really resign, as you'll see when you read them."

"WE WANT HARRY," the twins shouted and so David, not knowing quite what to say, smiled at Harriet and began to read:

First the title of the Club, then the members, then the names of the secret meeting places or headquarters, of which there were three – the original camp round the pine tree at Witchend, this barn at Seven Gates and the ruined castle at Clun where Jonathan and Penny Warrender had been enrolled.

The rules sounded a little childish:

Rule 1   The name is as above.
Rule 2   So are the members.
Rule 3   The Club and Camp are so private that every member swears in blood to keep them secret.
Rule 4   Every member promises to be kind to animals.
Rule 5   The Club is for exploring and watching birds and tracking strangers.

As David finished, Jenny gave a squeal of excitement.

"It's tracking strangers that's absolutely vital, Harry. I'd forgotten until this very minute something terrific I must tell you all. It's important because strangers are rare round here and I've seen the most wonderful, exciting and handsome stranger. Honest, I have — "

"All right, Jenny," David interrupted. "Tell us later. This is a solemn moment!"

"But I want Harriet to know about the sort of thing that can happen to us. This stranger might mean the start of a big adventure. Just listen for a moment, *please*. You want to hear about him, don't you, Peter?"

Peter looked startled and shook her head.

"Don't be silly, Jenny. Tell us later. Go on, David. Never mind the other rules because it's the oath that is really important, isn't it? Read the oath now and let Harry sign it if she agrees."

Jenny sulked and shrugged her shoulders dramatically as David turned the paper over and read:

"Every member of the Lone Pine Club signed below swears to keep the rules and to be true to each other whatever happens always."

"There you are, Harry. That's our oath. Read it over, and if you want to join us you must sign in your blood."

"Are you sure you've got any blood in you?" Dickie demanded. "You gotta be full-blooded to be a Lone Piner. You've gotta prick your finger with a needle and squeeze out the blood and use it like ink."

Then Harriet surprised them all.

"Don't be a silly little boy, Dickie. Of course I'll sign and thank you all very much for asking me to join. You and Mary seem to have forgotten that you made me an unofficial Lone Piner when we had that adventure in Yorkshire. You signed in blood too. Anyway, I'm the last Lone Piner and I'm glad, but I wish I'd been the first," and then she added: "Are you sure *you* want me, Jenny? I've got to know *now*."

For a moment Jenny looked ashamed.

"Yes, I do, Harry. I didn't want you before I met you, but hurry up now and sign and then I can tell you all about my romantic stranger."

So Harriet read the rules and the oath and then took the needle that Mary had borrowed from Trudie and without hesitation pricked the top of the middle finger of her left hand. She squeezed out a drop of blood and Dickie then passed her a sharpened matchstick. Harriet dipped the point in her blood several times before she was able to mark the paper – "H. Sparrow".

"Now I'm in at last," she laughed and then sucked her finger. "What happens now? Don't you tell me any of your most innermost secrets?"

"Only mine," Jenny said. "Listen, all of you. This morning, on the first bus, there came into our village the most handsome and romantic young man anybody in Barton has ever seen. He was a sort of hiker and he wants to explore the Stiperstones and the Mynd and he came into our shop and I was there. And he said, 'Hullo, young lady,' which was rather peculiar, but of course I said 'Good morning' very politely, but he was so handsome that my heart bumped and my voice got all squeaky which was *awful* . . ."

"What did he want and what did he say to you, Jenny?" Peter asked in a strained sort of voice.

"He wanted some postcards first and then he asked some most peculiar questions like how long had I lived in Barton and were my parents here during the war and was there anywhere he could stay while he was exploring and could Mum put him up which I knew she wouldn't but all the same he was so terrific and handsome and brown with very white teeth..."

She paused for breath and Dickie said:

"We're ashamed of you, Jenny. What *will* Tom say when we tell him?"

"I'll know what to say to Tom," Jenny laughed. "Anyway my handsome stranger said he'd like to talk to some other people in the village but he'd see me again sometime and when he got to the door what do you think he said?"

"That he was from outer space and would you go back with him to the moon in a spaceship," David suggested.

"Oh no. He wasn't a bit like a spaceman," Jenny replied. "He was too human. He said he liked girls with red hair."

Peter got up suddenly.

"You're absurd, Jenny. Really you are. It's getting too hot in here and I'm going to get some air."

She walked down the barn, and David, after a moment's hesitation, followed. Then the others got up as the doors were flung back, and at once Macbeth, the Scottie, dashed out into the darkness barking furiously.

"Like to come out for a bit, Peter?" David said quietly, but before she could answer they heard steps in the farmyard and a man's voice saying, "OK, dog. OK."

Then, into the pool of light at the threshold of the barn stepped a handsome young man with a rucksack on his back.

"Good evening," he said. "This looks like a party, but I hope some of you can help me. I've come a long way today and I'm looking for a bed." Then with a sudden smile of recognition. "Hullo, Peter. I told you we'd meet again soon."

CHAPTER 4

Fire!

The silence which followed the young man's reference to Peter was broken by the barking of Macbeth who pranced menacingly round the stranger's ankles as he slipped the rucksack from his shoulders.

Then, still looking at Peter, he said, "See to that dog, please. Call him off. He annoys me."

The twins, followed by Harriet and Jenny, stepped forward into the pool of light by the open doors and the latter gasped with surprise as David, after a puzzled look at the Peter, said:

"Be quiet, Mackie. Look after him, Mary," then to the newcomer, "Who are you and what are you doing here? Do you know him, Peter?"

Peter, angry because she was blushing, tried to explain.

"Not really. I met him this afternoon when I was sheltering from the storm at the ruined cottage under the mountain. Jenny knows the place, don't you?"

Jenny nodded. She had recognised the young man at once and was amazed that Peter, with plenty of opportunity, had not told her about this meeting.

"Yes, it's just off the road and part of the roof has fallen in, but half the stable is dry," Peter went on. "I left Sally there and ran into the house because by then I was just about wet through. And was I scared when I heard his step behind me! Jenny has always said the cottage is haunted and I nearly thought John was a ghost..."

Her voice broke as she met David's glance. She was thankful when John Smith tried to help her out.

"I wasn't a ghost and was nearly as wet through as Peter. I'd only been in the cottage a few minutes and was having a look round. You can be sure I was pleased to see her. She looked much too nice to be a ghost. My name really is John Smith, and as Peter doesn't seem to have had time to mention it, I'm on a hike through these hills because I'm reading geography at Birmingham University and I've got to write up the history of this district. I'm fascinated by this country and when Peter told me she had always lived round here I asked her to show me round. Now I'm tired and need a bed for the night. Didn't you say you'd got relations here, Peter? I hoped that they would be able to help me. Do you think I could rent a room here for a few nights?"

This speech was greeted with horrified silence, for not only were Charles and Trudie the last people to rent out a room to anybody, but there seemed something odd about the way John Smith suggested it. Then Macbeth began to bark again and Mary had to drag on his collar to hold him back.

"Can't any of you say anything?" Smith went on. "I'm quite harmless, but I'm very tired and hungry. Why don't you break up this kids' party and make room for me here?" Then he noticed Jenny. "Hullo, redhead. Haven't I seen you somewhere before?"

"Yes, you have. You came into my dad's shop in the village and asked a lot of questions and you told me that redheads were your favourite girls. And from what I hear you ask a lot of questions wherever you go. You're the romantic stranger everybody is talking about, but what a pity your name is John Smith. I think it ought to be Sebastian or Marmaduke or something out of a film like Carlo or Marlo. Shall we ask him in, David, and give him some cocoa and make him do some answering instead of asking?"

As usual, Jenny made everybody laugh – except the twins – and David replied:

"All right. You'd better come in, but it's a bit late asking for a bed, isn't it? Do you know where you are? And how did you get here? Not many strangers find their way up from the road to Seven Gates."

"But I'm not quite a stranger," John said as he heaved up his rucksack. "I'd already met Peter and she told me she was staying here. I'm serious about wanting information about this district and I particularly want to hear stories and the history of these hills. I hope some of you older ones can help me . . . This is a very unusual place. Do you all sleep here – and why are you having some sort of a kids' party?"

As he strolled into the barn, David suddenly hated his arrogance and slightly peculiar way of talking. He hated too the way in which he spoke of Peter with an easy familiarity. There was something altogether odd about his sudden appearance at this time of night. Then he noticed that Peter was already pouring cocoa into a mug, and Harriet brought it over to Smith who was now leaning against the table as if he owned the place.

As John Smith nodded his thanks, Mackie began to growl again and Mary released his collar. The little dog came forward, crouched and lowered his head on his front paws and went on growling. Peter, standing by the stove, said sharply, "Better tie him up, Mary. He's a nuisance tonight."

"No, he isn't," Mary said. "I'm sorry if that sounds rude, Petah, but he's a very good dog and it's not our fault if he doesn't like this new man. And which reminds us," she went on, speaking directly to John Smith, "I may as well tell you now that this isn't what you called a kids' party – "

"And if it was," Dickie added, "what we'd like to know is what is it to do with you if you know what I mean?"

"*He* knows what you mean, twin, and if he doesn't I'll

FIRE!

tell him again ... Acksherley, Mr Smith, if this is a party it's quite, quite private. And another thing. If you mean what we think you mean about 'older ones', then you'd better go away, even if you are a friend of Petah's."

"Which we doubt," Dickie added truimphantly.

For the first time John Smith looked annoyed, and David, watching him carefully, saw his grey eyes harden with dislike of the twins as they stood before him. Then he put his mug on the table and shrugged his shoulders.

"Stupid of me, I suppose, but I can't make out what these twins are talking about. Will one of you please call this dog off and then I'll try and explain myself again. I only want to be friendly, and as I don't really know my way around here, I was happy to meet Peter this afternoon. She was much nicer to me than any of you have been. I came up here because Peter told me it was a farm and sometimes farmers don't mind taking in guests for a night or two."

"This one minds," said Charles Sterling from the doorway. "Perhaps somebody will be good enough to tell me who this is? You're all making a lot of noise tonight and we think it's time you settled down."

Peter was the first to realise that Charles was really angry.

"We're sorry, Charles. We didn't realise that we were making a noise. This is John Smith. I met him this afternoon on my way here. He's hiking and he's looking for somewhere to sleep. John, this is my cousin, Charles Sterling."

John stepped forward.

"Good evening, sir. I hope you might be able to put me up, but if it's inconvenient —"

"I'm sorry. We don't let rooms here. Try the village: Jenny lives in Barton and may know somebody who does bed and breakfast. Now will you all settle down and be quiet. I've had enough trouble today one way and another, and I'd be glad if the young man will leave at once ... Good night."

They looked at each other in silence as Charles stalked across the farmyard.

John said:

"I don't seem to be very popular, do I? What about you, Jenny redhead? Do you know anybody who would have me in your village? You're not mad with me, are you?"

"Not really," Jenny admitted. "You're a mystery man though and I wish I knew why you came all this way through the whispering wood tonight."

Peter walked down the barn and closed the doors.

"I don't know what's come over us all and I can't understand Charles either," she said as she came back to the stove. "It's just ridiculous to expect John to walk down to Barton at this time of night. Why can't he sleep down here with David and Dickie, and we can talk it over in the morning? I can't understand why you wanted a room, John. You've got a sleeping-bag rolled up in your rucksack and the boys will show you where to get some hay for a mattress. Stay the night here, and at breakfast we'll tell you enough stories about these hills to make your hair curl. You agree, don't you, David? We can't turn him out tonight."

The others stared at her in surprise, but Harriet and Jenny were relieved at David's reply. The twins were not. They had already made up their minds about John Smith.

"OK then," David agreed. "There's plenty of room down here. But I don't think Charles is going to be very pleased if he finds out you've stayed here with us. Do you want to stop for the night, John? We're all tired and don't want to be gossiping here for hours."

"Thanks, David," John said. "I'd like to stay. I don't gossip and I don't believe I talk in my sleep."

"I bet you snore," Dickie said rudely. "If you wake

FIRE!

me up I shall set our dog on you. My twin and me don't like you. You're rude to Mackie and we think it most peculiar you coming here."

Once again John tried to keep his temper, but it was Jenny who saved the situation.

"Harry and Mary and me are going to bed anyway and please don't make a noise down here. Leave the washing up until the morning and please come up as quickly as you can, Peter."

"Yes, I will. I'm tired too. Show John where he's got to camp out, Dickie."

The three younger girls climbed the ladder to the old granary while Dickie, very grudgingly, showed John the storage compartment next to his own, which was generally used by Tom Ingles.

"Here's your dormitory, mate," he said. "There's a bundle of hay in the corner and please don't make a noise chewing it," and then he found himself lifted off the floor, shaken till his teeth rattled and dumped on the bale of hay in the corner. This rude treatment surprised him very much, and he was too chastened to answer back when his brother said, "Serve you right, Dickie. You're too cheeky tonight. Shut up and go to bed."

"Let's go outside," Peter suggested. "The stove is nearly out, but it's still hot in here. I'll go up when the others have settled down. There's not room up there for four girls to get into sleeping bags at the same time."

John and David followed her out into the farmyard again. There were no lights in the house and no sound broke the silence of the night. Then John began to ask questions about who was here in the Second World War and did they know anybody who was actually living in the hills at that time.

"You'd better keep your voice down," David whispered. "We don't want Mr Sterling to know you're

NOT SCARLET BUT GOLD

still here. Why are you so interested in what happened here in the war? Who cares now, anyway?"

John was obviously trying so hard to be pleasant that Peter was annoyed with David, who was now being as ungracious as Dickie was rude. He was showing up badly and she suddenly felt miserable.

"I've got my reasons for asking," John said quietly. "I want to find someone old enough to remember a long way back. That's the way you find out about places . . . Would you like to walk down through the wood with me, Peter? I don't think David likes me much more than those twins."

Peter heard David draw in his breath sharply.

"Oh, don't be silly, John," she whispered. "It's much too late for a walk, and anyway I'm tired and going to bed now. Good night, both. See you in the morning."

The farmyard was moonlit now and when she looked back John and David were glaring at each other.

There was no sound from Dickie as she lifted her torch from the hook just inside the door and tiptoed across to the ladder leading to the granary. She was too unhappy to talk to anybody and hoped the others were asleep by now.

The window was outlined by the pale moonlight as she stepped over Harriet and Mary in their sleeping-bags. She flicked on her torch for a moment to see whether Jenny had left her space to undress, and saw Mackie curled up against Mary. Neither of the two younger girls stirred, but Jenny, who always slept as close to Peter as she could because she enjoyed a gossip, was awake.

"Get into your bag soon as you can, Peter," she whispered. "I want to talk to you."

"*Please*, Jenny. I'm too tired to talk."

Jenny sniffed and fidgeted while Peter undressed in the dark and struggled into her pyjamas. The hay in her mattress rustled but smelled very sweet as she zipped herself into her sleeping-bag and snuggled into its warmth.

"Peter," Jenny whispered a few inches away. "*Peter*. Don't be mad with me, but why don't you tell me what's wrong? You can trust *me*. I've always been your friend and you were really the first friend I ever had. Do you remember? You're unhappy, aren't you?"

"I know I'm being horrid to you, Jenny, but please go to sleep. I don't want to talk now but I will tomorrow. Honest I will, and I know you're a good friend. I've had a beastly day, but perhaps everything will be better tomorrow."

Jenny murmured, "Good night. God bless then. Sleep well."

But Peter couldn't sleep. First she heard the sound of cinders falling in the stove below and then footsteps and the mutter of voices as David and John came in. They were quiet enough after that, but all the memories of this unhappy day came crowding back. She turned over so that she could see out of the window but could get no peace. She thought of her father and the way he had broken the news of their move, of her unhappiness over David and the odd way in which he was behaving. Certainly he had been jealous just now, but that didn't explain why he had written to Jenny instead of to her and why he had been so cool since they had met this evening. Everything seems magnified when you can't sleep and she was also puzzled about Charles and Trudie. She did hope that they hadn't squabbled, but she had never known Charles so bad-tempered as he had been over John just now. And he'd said something about having plenty of trouble too, which wasn't like him. And why had he been so rude to John? Why was everybody – except Jenny perhaps – rude to John?

Dickie had been much worse than usual with a stranger. And Mackie too had obviously disliked him.

At last Peter slept but even her dreams were of the handsome stranger who wanted to know so much and who so obviously admired her.

She slept while the moon climbed up the sky; while Macbeth, at Mary's side, stirred, whined and then growled softly; she slept without hearing a footstep below and the creak of a door.

Later, Macbeth whined again and Peter woke up with thumping heart and the feeling that something was wrong. Macbeth whined again and ran over to the window, the bottom of which was at floor level. Peter, with a hand on his collar, turned over to look out over the moonlit farmyard. It was as she had often seen it. Still and quiet. But Mackie seemed uneasy and Peter was sure that something unusual had wakened him.

"What is it, Mackie?" she whispered.

She knelt up so that she could look above the tree-tops and saw a red flicker reflected in the sky.

"Jenny! Jenny! Wake up!" she shouted as she scrambled out of the sleeping-bag and reached for her jeans. "Get up! There's a fire on the farm. Wake the others. I must warn Charles and get the boys up."

Macbeth began to bark but Jenny was out of her bag and shaking Harriet by the time Peter had pulled a sweater over her head, switched on her torch and was climbing down the ladder. She dashed down the barn shouting, "Wake up, David! Fire! Fire!" and then ran into his cubicle, shone the torch in his face, grabbed his hair and shook him awake. It was not surprising that he woke in a temper and, without realising who was hurting him, got an arm out of his sleeping-bag, swung up his fist and hit the side of her head.

"You beast, David!" she shouted. "Get up! Get the

FIRE!

others up and come and help. There's a fire below the wood and I must wake Charles."

She found her shoes, grabbed her jacket and struggled with the great doors. As she got them open and swung the beam of her torch into the darkness, she saw David in pyjamas, with his jeans in one hand, rubbing his head with the other.

"Coming, Pete!" he shouted.

She ran across the farmyard and found to her surprise that the back door of the house was locked. Whenever the Lone Piners were using the barn, Charles and Trudie left this door open in case any of them wanted to come into the house during the night, and it was unusual for Charles not to tell them that he was going to lock up. As she banged the heavy, old-fashioned knocker, Peter remembered again that Charles had said something about having plenty of trouble today.

She went on banging until some lights came up in the house and Charles opened the door.

"Peter! What's wrong? What's all the row about?"

She told him. "It's your Dutch barn in the field below the wood, I think. I saw the reflection from the granary window. Hurry, Charles."

He swore. "It's the hay, I reckon. Don't go down there alone. Wait for me."

She heard him shouting to Trudie upstairs, then down he came again with trousers and sweater over his pyjamas. He cursed as he struggled into his wellington boots.

"We must see how bad it is before we telephone for the fire brigade ... Tell your lot to bring hay rakes and pitchforks from your barn – they're stored in the cubicle nearest the door ... I'm going ahead."

As Peter followed Charles out into the moonlight, the yard was suddenly full of Lone Piners. They streamed back into the barn for rakes and pitchforks and then ran like a rabble down the slippery track between the trees. It was dark in the wood, and the twins, being the smallest, found the rakes difficult to manage. Dickie fell twice and Mary tripped up Harriet, and when these three arrived in the field the others were already pulling out lumps of glowing, smoking hay stored under the roof of an open-sided Dutch barn.

"See that empty petrol can," David gasped to Charles as together they forked out another red-hot bale and flung it behind them on to the damp grass. "Somebody's fired your ricks deliberately. Do you want the fire brigade? We can cope, can't we?"

Charles looked round at the others, dancing like smoky little devils in the moonlight, breaking up the smouldering bales and then stamping out the embers.

"We've beaten it already, David, thanks to Peter. Baled hay doesn't burn easily and what she must have seen was the petrol flames when the fire was started ... No need to fetch the brigade unless the wind gets up."

Ten minutes later the fire was out but nearly a third of the precious hay was ruined. "All up to the house," Charles ordered as he wiped the perspiration in streaks from his blackened face. As they trudged up the hill again, David realised that Peter was beside him.

"That was smart work, Pete. What made you wake up?"

"I'm not sure. Mackie must have heard something ... David. Where's John? Didn't you wake him?"

"Not specially. After you'd gone over to the house I lit one of the lanterns and shouted to him and Dickie. Then I forgot him, I suppose. Perhaps he prefers to have his sleep out. He said he was tired. Or maybe I thought you'd wakened him first?"

"David! What a foul thing to say. I woke the girls and then called you. I can't think what's come over you."

"Neither can I," David muttered as she hurried ahead.

Trudie met them in the farmyard.

"OK, darling," Charles called. "All safe now, but it would have been much worse except for Peter and the others. It's a job for the police, of course. The ricks were fired with petrol taken from our store, and we think we know who's responsible, don't we?"

"Oh, surely not, Charles! How horrible . . . Anyway you must all come into the kitchen and clean yourselves up and have some tea."

When they were all together in the kitchen the clock showed twenty minutes past three. Trudie poured tea from an enormous pot and Peter passed round biscuits.

Charles thanked them again. ". . . And I may as well tell you now that I think I know who fired the ricks and warn you that there's going to be trouble. No, Trudie. They must know what happened today . . . For a week or two I've had a young chap working here called Jem Clark. He looks a doubtful character and lives in a cottage with his mother over the other side of the mountain. You must know it, Jenny. Stands by itself up a track about a quarter of a mile from the road. Jem hasn't got a father and he's not much good. I wish I'd never taken him on, for he's made nothing but trouble since he's been here."

"He's got a big black motorbike," Jenny put in. "He's been in trouble in Barton too: my dad says he stole some pens out of his shop once. Nobody sees Mrs Clark much except on the Shrewsbury bus sometimes. I know where they live but it's so lonely up there that nobody ever sees them. I wouldn't go there by myself."

"Those are the people, Jenny. I thought you'd know them. Anyway, I sacked Jem yesterday because he's no idea of regular work and comes and goes when he likes. He was very impertinent and came back today when I was at market and was rude to Trudie. She got rid of him without much trouble, but he went off threatening us both, and so you see why I think I know who stole my petrol and fired the hay. I shall decide what to do in the morning, but I'm worried about something else. Do any of you know anything more about that cool young customer who was asking for a bed here? He said he knew you, Peter. When did he go and why do you think he came to Seven Gates?"

Peter flushed. "I told you, Charles, that I met him this afternoon when I was sheltering from the rain. He's from Birmingham University and on a walking holiday and he's got to write an essay or something on the hills round here. I told him I was staying here with friends and as, I suppose, he couldn't get a bed in Barton he tried here... And please don't all stare at me. Why shouldn't he? He was polite and friendly and I liked him."

"Nobody is staring at you, darling," Trudie said. "Charles told me about him, but you didn't. When did he go?"

"I don't know," Peter said defiantly. "I asked him to stay and the others agreed. He slept down with the boys, next to Dickie, I suppose. I didn't wake him specially when I saw the fire. I called David and ran over here, but I don't think any of us have seen him since."

"I thought I told him to clear out," Charles said with a hard edge to his voice. "This isn't like you, Peter. You've disobeyed me. I'm responsible for all of you and I don't want strangers round the place. I credited you with more sense. You too, David. Do you know when he went?"

"No, Charles, I don't. I admit I didn't realise that he wasn't with us when we ran down to the fire. I suppose he went before Peter gave the warning – but I can't be sure. He may have cleared out as soon as we were out of the way. I just don't know."

"I looked in the barn just now," Peter admitted. "All

his things have gone. I'm sorry, Charles, if we've disobeyed you. I was sorry for him because he's nowhere to sleep. All my fault, I suppose. Mackie was very restless and he may have heard him moving about downstairs . . . Anyway, I'm sure John didn't have anything to do with the fire."

"How can you be sure?" Charles snapped. "You know nothing about him except that he can't seem to mind his own business. Why, after asking for and getting hospitality, should he clear out suddenly and secretly without a word of thanks?"

"I expect he went because he was sure that he wasn't welcome," Peter replied and, with her head held high, she walked out of the kitchen.

CHAPTER 5

The Patchwork Quilt

Between the lower, western slopes of the Stiperstones and two mountains called Corndon and Stapely is a stretch of desolate country called by some the "Land of Dereliction." It is well named, for from the heather of this lonely moorland, treacherous with bogs, the gaunt arms of ruined mineshafts rise through the mist above slag-heaps and pools of stagnant water. The Romans mined all this land for lead long, long before miners came back, in the last century, to this haunted corner of Shropshire. These later miners tore up the earth, built engine houses, sank shafts and buried the golden gorse under piles of rubbish.

Those were hard days in a hard country and it must have been about that time that a few shepherds, some perhaps with the courage of despair, made their homes on the lower slopes of the Stiperstones. Most of these cottages were now piles of rubble through which the heather thrust its tough, triumphant stalks. But there was one still in good repair, not far from the lonely road to Snailbeach and Minsterley which skirts the flanks of the Stiperstones past some mine workings.

This cottage was the home of the widow Clark and her son Jem and she had lived there for as long as most people could remember. She was a woman who never cared what others thought of her, for here, somehow or other, she had managed to bring up her only son and, as country people say, "kept herself to herself".

At about ten o'clock on the morning after the fire at Seven Gates, Kate Clark opened the door of her cottage and looked down the rough track through the

THE PATCHWORK QUILT

heather to the road. Only now was the sun dispersing the mist which lay like a blanket over the Land of Dereliction, and when she looked up at the mountain behind her she was not surprised to see that the Devil's Chair was still hidden in the clouds.

She stood for a moment or two, listening, but the only sound was the haunting cry of a curlew and this was nothing unusual to her. She was wearing a shabby black dress and a red cardigan over a flowered apron. Her hair, except for an unusual wide streak of white in it, was as black as her piercing eyes, and although her shoulders were stooped she was still good-looking. She went into a lean-to shed to collect firewood, and while she was there a man with a heavy pack on his back came into sight on the road. By the time Kate came out of the shed, her apron filled with kindling, the stranger had reached the track leading to the cottage.

They saw each other at the same moment, although they were two hundred yards apart. Kate's heart thudded with surprise as the man left the road and started up the track towards her. She hated strangers, and as Jem had not been home for two nights and had sent no message, she was suddenly afraid.

When the stranger saw her waiting at the open door he raised his hand in greeting. Kate could see that he was young and there was something about him which disturbed her. He strode easily up the rough path and as he approached she wondered whether she had seen him before. There was something in the way he carried his head; and the way he looked at her, with a slight smile on his handsome face, set her heart thumping. She leaned against the doorpost and dropped the firewood from her apron. Above the roaring in her ears she could hear the clink of his shoes against the loose stones, and she did not realise that she was staring at him open-mouthed, as if he was a ghost, as he smiled and said, "Good morning. You are Mrs Clark? I've come a long way to see you and I hope you can help me."

Suddenly she felt a stab of pain about her heart, and as his face came nearer and nearer she fell in a faint across her doorstep. Vaguely she felt herself lifted, carried and lowered into her own rocking-chair in her own kitchen and then the shock of cold water flung in her face brought her back to reality. The young man, with an empty mug in his hand, was smiling at her.

"Sorry about that, Mrs Clark. Are you feeling better? What happened?"

"Who are you?" she gasped as she wiped the water from her face. "Who *are* you? What do you want?"

"I'll tell you when you're feeling better," he said. "What you want is a cup of tea and if you'll sit there quietly I'll make you one. Don't worry. I'll find my way about."

He did so competently. A big, smoke-black kettle was already singing on the kitchen range, and teapot and tea were within reach. He fetched the wood from the doorstep to brighten up the fire and the kettle was soon boiling. He made the tea and poured out a cup for himself as well as for her. She took it gratefully.

"Tell me who you are and why you've come," she whispered. "How do you know my name? Did my son send you?"

There was a gleam of excitement in his eye as he leaned forward in his chair and talked to her. He had great charm and was very strong-willed. She was unhappy, bewildered by what had happened and still dizzy with shock, but his story rang true. He was a student from Birmingham, exploring this district as part of his studies, and had been sleeping out. He said that he did not know her son, but had been told that she had

THE PATCHWORK QUILT

lived here for a long time and was likely to know all the stories and legends about these hills.

"That's why I've come to see *you*, Mrs Clark. Will you let me stay here for a few days? I can pay you well, but I'm tired and hungry and if you don't take me in I don't know who will. I tried Barton, but nobody there wants me. I don't mind living rough, but although I'll be out exploring most of the day I want a roof over my head when I come back, and something hot to eat. And I want you to tell me about these hills, too. You won't turn me away like the others, will you?"

She cowered back as she whispered:

"No. No. You can't stay here. Nobody stays here. There's only one other room besides mine and that's my son's. He's away today, but he'll be back soon . . . He wouldn't like anyone else here. We don't like strangers. I'm sorry I come over funny, but I'm all right now. Thank you for your help and for making the tea . . . You'd better be on your way now."

He ignored this suggestion.

"Mrs Clark, I've slept out and have had no breakfast. I'm hungry and too tired to go farther. If you're really feeling better, will you please sell me a meal? You're not the sort of woman to turn away a man when he's hungry. I know you're not. Suppose *your* son was tired and hungry and went to a house for help and was refused. Just think of that, Mrs Clark. You wouldn't like that, would you?"

She looked up and met his compelling eyes. Once again she felt a sudden sense of shock. He was too strong for her.

"You may bide for an hour," she said briefly as she got up. "There's not much food, but you're welcome to some bread and cheese. Sit here if you're that tired and I'll make a fresh brew of tea."

He made himself comfortable, and as she busied herself getting him something to eat he was sure that he had won her over. He believed it to be only a matter of time and patience, and so it proved. When she had made some more tea he thanked her again.

She clasped her cup with both hands and watched him with frightened, bright, expectant eyes. He too shared something of this excitement and it was not long before she began to talk more freely. He asked her first about her son and soon guessed correctly that, although he was the centre of her life, she was also afraid of him.

"He's a lucky boy, Mrs Clark. Lucky to be looked after by a mother like you, I mean. Where is he?"

"He's no boy. He's a man now. Your age too, I shouldn't wonder . . . He's away now, but he'll be back today like as not. That's why you can't stay here."

It was not very difficult after that to get her to admit that her son was born here, in this cottage, after her husband had been killed, and that she had never left it.

Then it was that John Smith, by his will and personality, forced this odd, lonely woman back into the past. He soon realised that he had some power over her, for she could not take her eyes from him.

"So you were here all through the war, Mrs Clark? These hills are lonely enough now, but you must often have been frightened then. How did you get food? Weren't you scared to live here alone?"

He was both patient and clever and it was not long before she was telling him the greatest secret in her life – a story she had never told another soul, not even her son. She sat in her old rocking-chair, the back of which was covered with a gay patchwork quilt, and with her work-grimed fingers gripped together in her lap she told her strange story as if it were a relief to share it.

Johann Schmidt listened with rising excitement

which he dared not show.

"No, I wasn't all that scared to be living here in the war. They could get on with their war. Although there was the rations which I had to fetch, I had a cow here. We managed and, war or no war, the hills don't change. I got no time for the war. Silly lot o' fools, all of them."

"But didn't you have some soldiers over the mountain, Mrs Clark?"

"Soldiers is only ordinary men. Most of 'em would rather be home. O' course we had the Home Guard to look after us, but they was all blokes we knew . . . And the police. They came regular. Asking nosy questions. Nag, nag . . . I don't like policemen. Never have. And they never got the better of Kate Clark."

"No, Mrs Clark. I don't suppose they would. I've heard stories about German spies being landed on the mountain. I suppose that's why the police came regularly. Did you ever see any spies?"

Suddenly her hands gripped the arms of her chair.

"You'd best go now, young man. I won't have you here when my son comes home and you're asking too many questions. What would I know or care about spies? I'll not be charging you for the bread and cheese, but I'll be glad if you'll go now."

John got up. From his shirt pocket he took the letter given to him by his uncle, and a faded photograph. Without glancing at the latter he passed it over.

"Look at that face carefully, Mrs Clark. Have you ever seen that man? He is my father, but I cannot remember him. *Look carefully.*"

As if hypnotised she took the photograph in shaking fingers. The blood drained from her face again and she dropped the print in her lap.

"I knew it," she whispered. "You're his son! He told me he had a son. I could see him again as you came up the track ... After all these years I saw him again."

Not too gently he took her hands from her face.

"Now!" he whispered urgently. "Now, Mrs Clark. Now you will tell me everything about my father."

She told him all that she knew. She told him how one dark, cold night she had been wakened by a knocking on the cottage door and a weak cry for help. She told him that the stranger was wet through and delirious with fever. He didn't know what he was saying and collapsed on the floor as soon as she closed the door. She didn't know who he was, but how could she turn him away on such a night? She though he was dying, but she put him into this very rocking-chair and somehow got his clothes off him, although he struggled to keep his jacket. She dried him, warmed him by the fire and gave him hot milk. And, in time, she got him upstairs and into the small bedroom next to her own and there she wrapped him in blankets. Next day he was a little better – well enough to beg her not to let anybody know that he was here – and she'd promised to keep his secret. Then one day a policeman had come and asked if she'd seen any strangers, because they believed that German spies had been dropped by parachute on the Devil's Mountain and the Long Mynd. She had lied and said she's seen nobody, but if she did she'd get a message to the police who would be coming to see her regularly.

No, she told John. No, she hadn't asked the man upstairs if he was a German spy. She didn't care whether he was or not. It was nothing to her. She did not even know his name. He was ill and in trouble and he'd asked for help and she'd given it, and he was the kindest, gentlest man she had ever known.

"But what happened to him? Tell me, Mrs Clark!"

"I don't know. Soon after the policeman had been the

first time he just went and took all his things with him. I'd been to the village. I had to go sometimes and leave him. When I got back he'd gone, and what could I do?"

"Wasn't there a message? No message for you? No message for anybody?"

She shook her head.

"Nothing. He'd made his bed though. He'd do anything to help me, but he was ill. Sometimes he didn't know what he was saying. Sometimes then he used words I couldn't understand. Another language maybe."

As she talked, tears trickled down her face.

"But why did he go, Mrs Clark? Why was he such a fool to run off from here when he was safe?"

"He was no fool, lad. He was the finest man I've ever known and he went because I told him about the policeman. He went because he believed that Jem and I would be in trouble if anybody found out I'd been looking after him. He did it to help us, but he was ill and weak and the fever hadn't gone . . . He went and I never heard any more. Sometimes I've thought it was all a dream and that's why I came over funny when I saw you coming up the path. The dream come true, you see. Now I know it wasn't a dream . . ."

John gripped her hands so hard that she winced with the pain. His eyes were blazing with excitement.

"But you must know something. Was he never found? What about his body?"

The tears were still on her face as she struggled.

"I don't know any more. I think he went on the mountain to die. There's plenty of caves – many secret places."

"But he must have left some message. Didn't he leave a paper? Didn't he promise you money if you helped him?"

"Money? There was no money between us."

NOT SCARLET BUT GOLD

"Think! Think, woman! For God's sake try and remember. Wasn't there anything that he said that puzzled you? Did you search his room?"

She begged him to go then, and he changed his tactics.

"Now, Mrs Clark, I'm sorry if I've upset you but I'm upset too. This man you helped was my father and even if you *didn't* think we were alike I can prove it with this letter. I believe that my father left a lot of money somewhere in these hills. He probably hid it before he came here on that stormy night. If you will help me to find this money, I will give you a share. You could make good use of money now, I expect."

"I couldn't do that," she whispered. "I don't know where to look. I don't ever go out on the mountain. I don't want anything to do with it."

He paced up and down the room shouting at her.

"You *knew* my father. You helped him when he was in trouble. Why won't you help me? Can't you remember *anything* he said that will help me? You can read this letter from my father which was only given to me on my birthday a few weeks ago. He *tells* me that if he didn't come back from the war there might be money in these hills for me to find. *I'm sure it's hidden somewhere round here* and I've come to find it. Think again, Mrs Clark. You liked my father. He would want you to help me. Can't you remember anything that will help us? *Think!*"

"Yes," she whispered. "Yes. I believe that you're his son and I don't want to read the letter. He'd want me to help you ... Yes. There was one thing he kept saying in his fever. Silly it was. So silly that I wrote it down."

John wheeled on her. He had not noticed that the cottage door was still half open, nor did he hear the sound of footsteps on the path. "Tell me!" he shouted. "I'm not leaving here until I know. *I've got to know!*"

68

CHAPTER 6

Not Scarlet But Gold

"I don't care how stupid it was!" John shouted. "Tell me what he said. I've got to know and I'm not leaving here until you tell me."

She didn't answer because she was watching the half-open door. There was a sharp knock and it swung back to disclose Charles Sterling looking very angry.

"Good morning, Mrs Clark. I've come to see Jem. Have you seen him?"

Then he recognised John and gave him a surprised nod.

"Is Jem here, Mrs Clark?"

"No, sir. I don't know where he is. I was thinking of coming over to Seven Gates to ask you. He's not been home for two nights and his motorbike is not here either. I hope he's not in trouble, sir."

Charles Sterling stepped into the room. He looked meaningly at John, who stared at him coolly. "I'll come in, if you please, Mrs Clark. I've got something private to say to you. Perhaps you'll wait outside, young man, but I'd like a word with you too before I go."

"That's OK, Mr Sterling," John said. "Don't disturb yourself. I'm living here at present and looking after Mrs Clark. *You'd* like me to stay, wouldn't you, Mrs Clark?"

"I'm sure I don't mind. I only want to know what's happened to my Jem. Sometimes he sends me a word or a message if he's going to be away, but I haven't heard anything of him for two days past. Have you brought bad news, sir?"

John showed no intention of moving, so there was nothing else Charles could do but ignore him.

"I'm not sure whether you'll think it bad news, Mrs Clark, but I'm going to tell you the truth. I sacked Jem two days ago and packed him off right away with an extra week's money. He's a troublemaker, a bad timekeeper and impertinent. Late last night somebody set my hay afire in the Dutch barn. I want to ask Jem a few questions, and if he doesn't come up to the farm to see me within the next twenty-four hours I'm going to make trouble for him."

Mrs Clark stood up.

"Oh no, sir. You're wrong about Jem. He's a wilful lad, I know, and a bit wild, but he wouldn't set hay afire. I was sure that he was going to settle down at Seven Gates, sir."

"I wasn't so sure, Mrs Clark, and I hope for your sake that he'll keep out of more trouble," Charles said, and he turned to John.

"I've forgotten your name, but I know you were in my barn for a while last night against my orders. I believe you'd left before the youngsters gave the fire alarm. Do you know anything about that fire? Where were you last night after you left my farm?"

"I need not answer your questions, Mr Sterling, but I did not fire your hay. Why should I? Although you were rude to me, I decided that I wouldn't embarrass my friend Peter by staying in your barn with those children. I'm used to sleeping out rough and I know when I'm not welcome. You made that very clear last night, and I can't think why."

"Very well," Charles said. "I'm not sure what you meant about your 'friend' Peter, who is my cousin, but you can be sure now that you'll be even less welcome at Seven Gates in future than you were last night. Keep away, if you please. As for you, Mrs Clark, I'm sorry if you didn't know I'd sacked Jem, but I tell you now that

NOT SCARLET BUT GOLD

if he hasn't come up to see me by this time tomorrow I shall put the police after him . . . You and your friend here had better find him. I heard this chap threatening you when I came up the path. Nothing to do with me, but I'd send him packing if I were you . . . Good morning."

John followed him to the door and stood on the steps, watching him walk down the track. Not until the farmer had driven away did he turn back into the cottage and shut the door behind him.

"Now, Mrs Clark. We must arrange things quickly. Tell me now what my father said that you thought was so silly. I've got to know."

He stood over her and forced her back into her chair.

"No," she said suddenly. "You're threatening me and I won't be bullied. You must go away. I don't want anything to do with you. I don't care if you are his son, for you've brought nothing but trouble since you came here. You've had your breakfast and now you can go."

Then he told her that Jem was going to be accused of firing the hay, and unless she told him what he wanted to know he'd go to the police now and start them hunting for him.

"They'll get him, Mrs Clark, and I'm not sure what this might mean for him. You must be sensible and tell me what my father said. The silly thing you wrote down because you wanted to remember it. Just tell me and I'll leave you alone. I'll go away if you like and I won't tell them about Jem, but *I've got to know what my father said.*"

She gave in. She was miserable and upset by the memories this young man had brought back to her.

"Very well," she said. "Just listen to what I say and then go . . . I told you that your father had a fever. He was very ill and he talked much nonsense. Words in his own language that meant naught to me and words in

English which didn't mean much more. I remember as if it was yesterday, though, that he whispered again and again . . . *'Not scarlet but gold . . . That's the way to remember it. Not scarlet but gold.'* That's what he said."

He gripped her shoulders so that she cried out.

"You're making it all up," he stormed. "I've never heard such silliness. What you call nonsense . . . That is it. Nonsense it is, as you say. You are making it up."

She twisted her shoulders away from his cruel hands, and even in her pain and misery she realised that his words and phrases suggested that he was not English.

"I am not making it up," she said quietly, "and I can prove it. Those words are what your father said many, many times. *Not scarlet but gold.*"

"But what did he mean? Did you never try to find out what he was talking about?"

"No," she said simply. "No, I did not. He was too ill. Half the time he did not know what he was saying, and when he was clear in the head I did not wish to remind him of when he was ill. Why should I?"

"You're an old fool!" he shouted. "I don't believe you. You've made up this nonsense about scarlet and gold just because you want to get rid of me."

Then, to his surprise, Mrs Clark recovered some courage and dignity. She stood up and faced him.

"Now look here, young man. I believe you to be the son of the man I sheltered here all those years ago. He was a fine man and kind to me. You look like him and there's something in your voice which reminds me of him. And that's about all you've got of him. You've got no manners and you're trying to bully an old woman. You say what I've told you is a lie, but I can prove I'm right. I'll show you and then you can go."

She picked up the patchwork quilt from the rocking-chair. It was a cheerful quilt made up of six-sided pieces of different coloured materials all stitched together and lined with a piece of blue silk.

"Now keep quiet, young man, and listen to what I say for what I'm telling you is gospel truth. I was making this quilt when your father came to my door and you'd better know how I work it. Each piece of stuff has to be cut the same size, for it wouldn't look right if they was different shapes and sizes. The way to be sure is to cut pieces of brown paper the exact size you want and then use the paper as a pattern like, and cut the stuff around it."

"Mrs Clark," John said through clenched teeth. "I don't care how you made it. *Will you get on and prove to me what my father said?*"

"You've got a lot to learn, young man, and patience is the first thing. If you look at this quilt, you'll see there's plenty of red and yellow patches. I was sitting by your father's bed when I was making this quilt. He was that ill that I didn't like to leave him when he was talking and shouting through his fever, and so this thing that he kept on saying I wrote down on some of my paper patterns and sewed them in the quilt. If you've got a knife you can unpick one of the yellow pieces now and see for yourself."

He took a knife from his pocket and did as she suggested. The stitches, considering their age, were still strong, but as he cut them through he felt paper between the yellow material and the lining. He ripped it out and saw that it was a piece of yellow newspaper.

"Try another," she said. "I used newspaper sometimes. See the date on it? War-time. And now we're talking it seems like yesterday. Try a red piece."

This time he was lucky. The paper was brown and still tough, and as he held it up to the light he saw a pencilled message in ill-formed capitals:

HE WANTS ME TO REMEMBER
NOT SCARLET BUT GOLD

She snatched it from him and said passionately. "There you are. It's true, but I don't know what it means. Maybe I should have asked him what he meant when he was better. I can't remember each day now, but I'm sure it was only a day or two after I wrote that on the paper that the police came for the first time and then he went. I don't know where, and as I know he's dead it doesn't matter any more. Oh, yes. He's dead. He'd have come back to see me else. Or sent me a word . . . Now I'm tired and feeling a bit funny again. You've upset me and I want you to go."

She sat back in the rocking-chair and closed her eyes. John tried again and again to make her say more but without success. Then he began to tear out more hexagons of silk from the patchwork and found another piece of brown paper with the same pencilled message. He was examining this when they heard a motorbike roaring up the track. Mrs Clark was hardly out of her chair when the door was flung open and her son Jem strode into the room.

He was wearing black jeans, high black boots and a black leather jacket, and his crash helmet was black with a red band round it. He was good-looking in a weak sort of way and it was at once obvious that he was in a furious temper. As his mother ran to him, he saw John and stepped back.

"Who's this?" he snapped. "What's going on here?"

His mother tried to explain while John stood by with a smug smile on his face.

"He's only a young man who lost his way, dearie. I've given him some breakfast and he's going now . . . You'll be wanting some breakfast yourself, I reckon, for you look tired out. Take off your coat and I'll make some more tea. Come along in."

Jem glanced at his mother almost as if she didn't exist and then flung his crash helmet into her chair. But he gave John a very different kind of look – angry and suspicious.

Then, "Right, mate! You can be on your way now. Have you paid for your meal? Settle up and get cracking."

John, who was again leaning casually against the table, watching Jem with half-closed eyes, did not change his expression at this rudeness. He was interested to see that Mrs Clark had bundled up the patchwork quilt with the loose pieces of paper and materials, so it was obvious that she didn't want her son to know about it. After a long pause he turned to her and said, "You'd better tell Jem about the message you've got for him from Mr Sterling, hadn't you?"

Jem turned on his mother.

"What's he mean? What message? What does this bloke know about Sterling?"

"Calm down, dearie. Don't fuss. I'll tell you presently. Take off your jacket. You're tired out."

John didn't change his position.

"Tell him that Sterling has accused him of setting fire to his hay and that unless he goes up to the farm to see him he's going to put the police after him tomorrow. Tell him that. He's got to know sometime, hasn't he?"

Jem whirled on him. "You liar! Get out!"

"I'm in no hurry. I've been wanting to meet Jem Clark. And I am not a liar. Your mother heard Sterling. So did I. I was here."

"Then Sterling's a liar. He's got a down on me."

"No, he isn't. I'm sorry about this, Mrs Clark, but you've got to know. Sterling was telling the truth. I saw Jem last night. He poured stolen petrol on the hay and I saw him fire it. I was going to sleep there."

Mother and son stared at him open-mouthed.

"So save your breath," John went on, speaking particularly to Jem. "I know you were there and I can report you as having come home here. I want your help and I can pay you for it. I can pay in money and pay by my silence . . . How well do you know these hills, Jem?"

For a moment Jem looked what he really was – a spoiled, greedy, boastful and selfish young bully. But he liked the idea of money and quickly made up his mind that it might be better to stay on the same side as this stranger who knew too much. He tried to recover his usual bounce and, typically, took no notice of his mother. "Of course I know these hills. Nobody better. Known them all my life and I can tell you that there's plenty to know. I've been here since I was a kid. What do you want?"

John stepped away from the table.

"We've got to move quickly, Jem. You work with me and when we find what I'm after and what's mine by right I'll pay you enough to get you out of this hovel if you want to. You won't have to look for work round here, I promise you. Do you know anywhere in the hills where we could hide . . . ? There's money in this, Jem. You going to help?"

Jem nodded and licked his lips. But neither of the two young men noticed the look of horror on Mrs Clark's face.

CHAPTER 7

"She Knows Too Much"

Harriet was the first of the Lone Piners to wake on the morning after the fire. She regarded her new friends affectionately as they slept. She had been looking forward for so long to coming to Shropshire, and now that she was actually here they seemed to be having an adventure within the first few hours. Mary and Dickie were just the same, of course, and Peter, although she was not quite as friendly as usual, was really just as nice. But Jenny? Harriet was sure that she was going to like Jenny very much. What could she do to make Jenny her friend?

Then she had her big idea. It must be past getting-up time, so perhaps she could give them all a surprise by going down to make some tea and start the breakfast. She managed to get into a sweater and jeans without making much noise, but as she was about to climb down the ladder she noticed that Jenny was awake. She put a finger to her lips, crawled over to her, and with her lips to her ear whispered. "Don't wake the others yet, Jenny. I'm going over to the house to make tea and start the breakfast. Why don't you come over too? Mrs Sterling won't mind, will she?"

Jenny snuggled her head into her pillow.

"I never, never, never want to wake up," she whispered.

The sun was pleasantly warm and chasing away the morning mists above the whispering wood when Harriet knocked on the kitchen door.

"Hullo, Harriet," Trudie said as she opened the door. "You don't have to knock. Lone Piners are always welcome. Are you the first up? We finished breakfast hours ago."

"I woke first, but Jenny is coming over soon, I think.

Would you mind if I made some tea for them? I thought I'd do that because I am a new girl, but I have met them all before except Jenny, you know."

"I know about you, Harriet. You've got some wonderful friends. Here comes Jenny yawning her head off and I'm going upstairs now, so you can have the kitchen to yourselves. Tell the others that Charles doesn't want any of you to go too far away exploring until he's seen Jem Clark. We don't want what happened yesterday to spoil your holiday, but be careful."

Then Jenny came in.

"Why did you get up early to do all this, Harry?"

"I wanted to give you all a surprise. Are you going to be friends, Jenny? I want to be, but I'm not sure if you like me."

Jenny flushed under her freckles.

"I wasn't sure either, but I believe I'm going to. Let's not worry about it, Harry, and then it's sure to happen. There's lots I want to tell you about and to show you, but let's have our tea first before we wake the others."

They could hear Trudie singing upstairs while Jenny did most of the talking. She told Harriet how wonderful Peter had always been to her, particularly when they had first met on the road to Barton Beach when she was unhappy at home and Seven Gates belonged to Charles' father.

"And now something awful has happened, Harry. It's something we've got to put right. You must have noticed that something is wrong between Peter and David. Peter promised last night that she'd talk to me about it, but whatever else we do this holiday we've got to make it right between them."

Harriet nodded wisely. She had never had a discussion like this before, but she could see that Jenny was serious.

"What about your handsome stranger, Jenny? Peter knew him, didn't she? D'you remember how she walked out of here last night saying that John had gone off because nobody made him welcome?"

Jenny frowned. "Yes, I do. When we all went up to bed you remember she wouldn't speak to any of us. I know she was only pretending to be asleep. We must all be specially nice to her, Harry. Will you help? If it's David's fault, Tom will have something to say to him. Now put those eggs on to boil and I'll go over and wake them up . . . That was fun, Harry. Thank you for asking me."

Breakfast in the big barn was not particularly cheerful because the twins wanted to discuss their heroism at last night's fire and Dickie, in spite of some frightening glares from Jenny, kept on introducing the subject of John and being rude about him. Harriet noticed, however, that Peter was always trying to change the subject. She was also glad to see that David and Peter had more to say to each other and were not as awkward together as they had been last evening.

When they were washing up and trying to decide how to spend the rest of the morning, Harriet gave them Charles' message. After some argument the twins persuaded Jenny to take them up the dingle so that Harriet could be introduced to the Devil's Chair. When Jenny realized that this would mean leaving Peter and David together, she supported the idea enthusiastically, pointing out that if four of them and Mackie went together they would come to no harm. Ten minutes later they went off, and David and Peter found themselves alone in the farmyard.

"I'm going to see Sally now. You can come if you like," said Peter.

He turned to follow her but before they reached the stable Charles Sterling drove into the yard.

"Hullo, you two. Where are the others?"

"They've only gone up Black Dingle," David said.

"They've got Mackie and they'll be all right together. Did you find Jem Clark?"

Charles got out of the car.

"No, I didn't. I've been to the cottage, but he's not there. His mother says he hasn't been back for two nights and I'm sure that she didn't know I'd sacked him, but I'm just as sure that she'd say anything to protect him. I'm worried about this business because there's something very odd going on. I may as well tell you, Peter, that that chap John Smith was there when I arrived and, what's more, he was threatening old Mrs Clark. I wish we knew more about this young man than you can tell us, Peter. I'm sure he's not straight, and what I don't like is that he was more than a match for me. He's a cool customer and said he was now living in the cottage. He also denied firing the hay, by the way, but he *could* have done it. Nobody knows where he spent the night after he left here, do they?"

"It's no good looking at me like that, Charles," Peter said indignantly. "Of course I don't know where he was or why he's gone to Mrs Clark's. I only met him yesterday and I still believe he told me the truth. You've all been very rude and unkind to him and, after all, it is possible that he's at the cottage just because he's got nowhere else to stay. Jenny told us that he'd been asking for a room in Barton without any luck and somebody might have sent him to Mrs Clark's. I think I shall ride over on Sally and ask him. He'll tell *me*."

"You'll do nothing of the sort," Charles said. "I don't like what's going on round here, but I've given young Jem twenty-four hours to report here before I put the police after him. If he's got any sense, he'll come, but whether he started that fire or not he's no good and I don't think John Smith is much better either. Try and forget the whole wretched business – and don't let the others go too far away from here . . . I'm going to see Trudie now."

"That's good advice, Peter," David said as the farmer went indoors. "Let's forget the whole business. I'd like to forget practically everything that has happened since we got here. Seven Gates isn't proving lucky for us this time, is it?"

"Then *why* did you come?" Peter asked angrily. "Why did you fix it without asking me? You wrote to Jenny but not to me, so it's not surprising that this isn't turning out to be lucky for either of us . . . No, David. Please don't say any more now. Haven't you enough sense to see that I'm upset and unhappy? I'm going to ride over on Sally to Mrs Clark's cottage and see what's going on."

"You can't do that after what Charles said!"

"Can't I? Who's going to stop me?"

"You just want to see that bloke John."

"Maybe I do. Maybe I've got several questions to ask him. Perhaps I want to see Mrs Clark too because I think Charles is in a temper and behaving very badly. He's just not being fair . . . And, anyway, if there's a mystery to clear up, I don't see why we shouldn't help. It's not so very long ago that *you* would have been the person to suggest that the Lone Piners took a hand instead of trying to forget all about it."

She turned and ran over to the stable. David, looking as hurt as if she had struck him, followed slowly.

"I'm sorry, Peter. Let's go over to the Clarks' cottage together. You could use Jenny's bike and I'll borrow one from one of the farm blokes. Let's go together and we'll talk this out. I'm sorry I said that about John. It's just that I don't understand what he's after and anyway, after what Charles said, I don't think you ought to go over there alone."

Peter wasn't so sure herself now, either, but she couldn't possibly explain to David that she wanted to see John again just to get him straight in her own mind. Neither was she going to give in now, so without saying more she saddled Sally and led her out into the farmyard. David, white-faced and angrier than she had ever seen him, stalked ahead and opened the gate for her.

"I'm sorry you don't want my company," he said, in a voice she didn't recognise. "You're just being stubborn and selfish and I hope you're not going to make a lot of trouble for other people. You don't need me to ask you to take care of yourself."

As the pony moved forward, Peter, with an impulse she could not explain, touched David's hair lightly as he stood with his back to the gate and smiled at him.

"Thank you for offering to come. I'll take care, but this is something I want to do by myself."

Sally was glad to be out of the stable and, as soon as they reached the road, cantered along the grass verge into Barton Beach. Once through the village the road climbed sharply through desolate country, with the huge flanks of the Stiperstones on the right. The higher Peter rode, the more nervous she became, for she knew now that she was silly to have come alone. It was not too late to turn back, but it would be difficult to confess to David that he had been right!

She rode on and presently came to the wood that masked the entrance to Greystone Dingle where they had once had an adventure, and fifteen minutes later reached the highest point of the road before it fell away into the wastes of the Land of Dereliction. She checked Sally, who was pleased enough to nibble the grass at the wayside.

Although there was a little warmth in the spring sunshine, Peter suddenly shivered and set Sally trotting down through the heather at the side of the road. She had never before been to the Clarks' cottage but knew where to look for it. Soon she saw it standing, white-walled and four-square, a hundred yards or so back from the road and urged the pony into a canter. The sooner this expedition was over, the better!

Now she could see the path leading up to the cottage but no sign of life, until, on the faint breeze, she caught a whiff of wood smoke. Then, gathering her courage, she rode up to the cottage.

Peter slipped off Sally's back, looped her reins over a post and knocked on the half-open door. No answer.

"Are you there, Mrs Clark?" she called in a voice she did not recognise as her own. "May I come in?"

Then she thought she heard a muffled step from inside the house. Suddenly she was afraid. Scared to push back the door for fear of what she might see, and scared to be a coward and ride away from this haunted place never to return.

As she pushed the cottage door open, she remembered that David's last words to her after she had snubbed him were to take care of herself. The living-room was empty and untidy. A wood fire was still glowing in the old-fashioned range and across a rocking-chair was a pretty patchwork quilt from which a few of the shapes of coloured material had been cut. Some of these were on the floor. On the table was a brown teapot and some dirty crockery and when she looked at the clock she saw on the mantelpiece some hexagons of brown paper.

She stepped inside and called again:

"Mrs Clark! Please answer if you're here," and then she noticed some pencilled words on one of the scraps of paper: NOT SCARLET BUT GOLD.

She was so surprised that she picked it up – and at that moment heard the click of a latch. She turned to see a door in the corner of the room opening slowly.

An elderly woman with a white streak across her black hair was standing on the bottom step of a flight of stairs. She was twisting her hands in her apron and staring at her with frightened eyes.

"Go away," she whispered. "Go away at once. You can't stay here."

"Please don't be frightened of me, Mrs Clark," Peter said. "I've ridden over from Seven Gates. I heard that John Smith is here and I specially want to see him. Please tell me whether he is staying with you. My name is Petronella Sterling."

Mrs Clark came into the room, leaving the door to the stairway open behind her.

"You must go away," she insisted. "It's dangerous for you to come here and you must go before they come back. I don't know what they'd do if they found you here."

"But I'm not doing any harm, Mrs Clark. I only want to know about John Smith. I'm sure he's been here, but can't you tell me where he's gone or whether he's coming back? Why should I go?"

Mrs Clark grabbed her arm. "You've *got* to go. And I'm going too. They've made me go. I've lived here all my life, but now I've got to leave. I'm getting old now and they *make* me do things. *Don't you ever come here again.*"

Peter knew now that something was very wrong. There seemed no doubt that "they" must be Jem and John: but how had they got to know each other? And why was this rather pathetic woman so terrified? Peter glanced again at the mysterious shapes of paper on the mantelpiece. Mrs Clark, following her glance, snatched them up and stuffed them into the pocket of her dress.

"Don't tell them you saw," she whispered, "or it will be the worse for you. They don't mean anything, those scraps don't. Now go quick afore they come back and don't tell anybody you've been here . . . Get out. Quick."

Peter went. At the door she turned, trying to memorise everything in the room and it was then that she noticed three dirty cups on the table, which suggested that both Jem and John had been in the cottage.

Sally seemed as pleased to leave the place as her mistress, and they were nearly at the bottom of the stony track when they heard the roar of a motorbike. It was coming very fast, and even as Peter looked to the right down the road, the moving dot in the distance got bigger until she could see the black-clad driver crouched over the handlebars and another man on the pillion.

Jem and John without a doubt and perhaps it was as well that they hadn't caught her in the cottage. Peter turned Sally back the way they had come, but before the pony could settle into a trot the enormous bike pulled up with a screech of tyres, making Sally rear with fright and nearly throwing Peter. The driver pushed up his goggles and shouted above the roar of the engine.

"What were you doing up at the cottage? You've no right to be nosing about round here. Who are you?"

Peter, having calmed Sally, went white with rage and, as John Smith got off the pillion, shouted, "How dare you speak to me like that! Switch off that beastly engine and listen and I'll tell *you* something."

Rather to her surprise, Jem did so as she went on:

"Your friend Mr John Smith here will tell you who I am, but I know *you*. You're Jem Clark. I know you set fire to my cousin's hay last night. And it won't be long before a lot of other people know it too."

John, with a hard look on his face, came over and put a hand on Sally's bridle while Jem clutched his other arm.

"You heard that," the latter said menacingly. "I bet she's been up to the cottage nosing around and asking Mum questions. I don't care who she is. *She knows too much* and I reckon she ought to stick around here for a bit until we know what she's been up to."

"Be quiet, Clark," John ordered. "Leave this to me."

He looked up at Peter and smiled at her, but she knew this was not the same smile that had made her heart bump excitingly in the ruined cottage yesterday. The eyes were hard now.

"Now, Peter," he said quietly. "Tell me why you have come here? Was it to see *me*? I hope so. I didn't leave a message for you when I left the barn last night because I didn't know where I was going . . . You can still help me, Peter, as I asked you yesterday. Have you been up to the cottage and seen the old woman?"

While he was speaking, she watched him with astonishment and disgust. Now she knew that David's suspicions were justified. She remembered the frightened Mrs Clark in the cottage – the old woman who had been told to leave the home she had lived in for most of her life. This young man calling himself John Smith could not possibly be who he was pretending to be, and Peter was suddenly sure that whatever was happening was too big for her on her own. And she had been a fool to come.

"Well, Peter," John Smith repeated. "Do you want some fun and excitement with me? Not kid's stuff. Get off that pony and talk. I can deal with Jem Clark."

Her answer was to strike his hand from Sally's bridle. The pony reared again with surprise and then plunged forward, knocking John into the road. Over her shoulder Peter saw him scramble to his feet and shout something to Jem, who kicked his motorbike engine into life again.

As she guided Sally into the heather, she saw a familiar figure whizzing towards her down the hill on a bicycle. David! As Jem roared up the road, David braked, flung his bike into the heather and ran towards her. She turned Sally and rode to meet him.

"Follow me into the heather, David, if they come after us. They'll never catch us there. The one on the motorbike is Jem Clark."

David was fighting for breath and perspiration was streaming down his face as he leaned against Sally.

"You OK, Peter? Sure?"

"Yes. Yes, I'm all right, David, and I'm so sorry I – "

"Either of them hurt you?"

"Not really ... Here comes Jem. Be careful."

As David turned to face Jem, he said, "Ride Sally into the heather and keep out of the way of trouble. I'll cope with these two louts."

Jem stood his ground. David came up to him, noting that John was watching them from the road.

"So you're Jem Clark," David said, looking him up and down. "Mr Sterling has been looking for you and he'll be interested to know I've seen you. Staying here long?"

Jem began to swear. Peter was supposed to be out of earshot, but suddenly David lost his temper.

"Shut up!" he snapped. "Keep your dirty mouth shut or I'll knock you for six" – and at that moment nothing would have given him greater pleasure than to carry out his threat. And Jem knew it. He opened his mouth to swear again, thought better of it, turned his back and walked back to his motorbike.

David smiled grimly and then strolled over to Peter. She held out her hand and he took it in his.

"I'm sorry, David. I'm sure now that you were right about John. I've been an idiot. Thank you for coming to my rescue – or were you just going for a bike ride?"

"Just for a ride," he said grimly. "That's the sort of idiot I am. And you're crackers too. Sure neither of them touched you?" The motorbike had started again, but neither of them looked back at the road.

Peter shook her head. "No, David, but I was scared. There's something nasty happening and I've got a clue to the mystery. It's *not scarlet but gold* ..."

"My poor girl," said David. "You *are* crackers!"

CHAPTER 8

The Cave

When the twins with Harriet and Jenny got back to Seven Gates, after their expedition to the Devil's Chair, they were tired and rather bad-tempered. It had not been a successful trip because, although the twins wanted to impress Harriet with stories of their previous adventures on the Stiperstones, the latter had stuck close to Jenny and for much of the time the two elder girls had been talking about Peter. Then Mary had slipped and grazed her ankle and not even Dickie was particularly sympathetic. Harriet had climbed into the Devil's Chair, but Jenny refused and was scared when they heard the distant rumble of thunder.

"I know it's silly of me," Jenny said when Harriet clambered down again, "but I've never got used to this place. I'm sure the thunder means something horrid for us and I'm afraid it's to do with Peter and David. And why should Jem Clark hate Charles so much that he sets his hay on fire?"

Harriet was wondering why several unpleasant things should all happen on the first day of her real Lone Pine holiday and on the way down the dingle she walked with Mary, who was limping a little more than necessary. It was true that by the time they walked into the farmyard she was no longer limping.

The big white doors of the barn were open and Peter was lying in a deckchair on the threshold laughing – actually laughing – at David, who was sitting close to her on an old box.

"Something's happened," Jenny whispered to the others. "I believe they're OK with each other again."

Then she called to them. "Hullo! Have you two been there all morning? Have you got the dinner?"

Peter got up. "It can't be dinner-time yet. We've only just got back. We've had an adventure and David is crippled for ever. He rode somebody's ghastly old bike which was too big for him over to Mrs Clark's cottage and rescued me. We'll tell you all about it presently. Better have corned beef and bread and cheese."

"Ho! Ho!" Dickie said. "So you've both been slinking off and having an adventure while we've been looking after our new Lone Pine guest."

Peter laughed again. "Come on, Harry. We'll start on the dinner. You'd better find Charles, David, and tell him we've seen Jem and John Smith. And say I'm sorry I was so silly about John." David got up with difficulty and limped across the farmyard, holding his behind.

"What have you been doing to David?" Jenny asked Peter. "Except for his wounds he seems quite cheerful, which is more than either of you have looked since you got here."

"I've been a fool, Jenny," Peter said. "Come and help get the meal and we'll tell you everything."

Another thunderstorm broke while they were eating, and so they sat on round the table while Peter told them what had happened at the Clarks' cottage before David arrived on the borrowed bicycle. She didn't explain exactly why she had started off on Sally by herself, and the others had the sense not to ask.

"I was quite wrong about John Smith," she said. "And if you, Jenny, believe that redheads are his favourite girls I bet you're wrong too! His only favourites are those who do what he wants. What makes me so mad about the whole business is the way old Mrs Clark is being treated. She's terrified of that brute Jem and told me that she's got to leave the cottage. David believes, and so do I now, that John Smith is sure the Clarks have got something he wants. We think all his talk about hiking holidays and the paper he's going to write about the Shropshire hills is probably a bluff."

The thunder rolled and the rain poured down as they listened to her story of the patchwork quilt from which some hexagons had been cut, and of the pieces of paper on the mantelpiece and of Mrs Clark's panic when she realised she'd left them about.

"I've told David all this and I've shown him what I think may be a clue. You can all see it now. It's one of the scraps of paper which I'm sure were sewn into the quilt under the bits of silk and used as a sort of pattern. Maybe I was wrong, but I took one and here it is. The lettering is faint but clear enough."

Harriet, sitting next to her, took the scrap of paper.

"But it's very *old,*" she said. "And what does it mean? *Not scarlet but gold.*"

She passed the paper round to the others.

"It sounds royal," Mary suggested.

"It sounds silly," Dickie said. "Just a joke."

"Perhaps it's part of a love-letter," came from Jenny, and David asked sensibly, "Are you sure that all the other pieces had the same message, Peter? Do you think 'not scarlet but gold' is only part of a message?"

"I'm not sure. I think there were only three papers on the mantelpiece, and I picked this up from the floor when Mrs Clark grabbed the others. I believe the same words were on each, but for all I know every piece of the patchwork may have a message under it. Only a few of the patches had been cut out and Mrs Clark was obviously terrified because I'd seen them."

"Maybe," David broke in. "But from what you told me before, she was scared of Jem and John coming back while you were there and realising that you'd seen

THE CAVE

the quilt. My guess is that they're leaving the cottage because Jem started the fire and knows the police will be after him, and they dare not leave Mrs Clark behind for fear of what she'll give away. By what Peter and I saw of those two louts we think Jem has got something that John wants and John is the bloke who will give the orders. He's dangerous."

Then Harriet, flushed and excited, got up from the bench and said, "This is just about the most wonderful and exciting thing that has ever happened to me and, although I'm new, do you all mind if I say something? We'll never see the quilt again if Mrs Clark takes it wherever she goes, shall we?"

"Unless we send out Mackie to trail her down relentless," Dickie suggested.

"What I'm trying to say," Harriet persisted, "is that if the whole of the quilt wasn't ripped to pieces, perhaps the three of them know that 'not scarlet but gold' is the only message there. And if that's the truth then we know as much as the enemy, don't we?"

Peter shook her head. "Sorry, Harry, but we don't. We don't know what John is looking for. We can't even be sure that we've got the same clue, although I think we have. What did Charles say when you told him we'd seen the two together on the motorbike, David?"

"You'd better keep out of Charles' way for a bit, Peter. You're not his favourite girl, although I didn't tell him anything that happened. He said 'I told you so' about John Smith, but whether he really will tell the police about Jem tomorrow I don't know. I didn't want to say too much because we'd disobeyed him, but it's fairly obvious that Jem isn't going to come back here and own up like a naughty boy! I rather wish he would. I don't like him."

"My hero!" Peter exclaimed. "I must explain to the

others that you wanted to be really rough with him. I don't like him either because I'm sure he bullies his old mother and I'm sorry for her. I suppose Charles said none of us was to go near the cottage again?"

"He did. But perhaps that doesn't matter so much now if the three of them are leaving it. I want to find out about 'not scarlet but gold'. Anybody got any ideas? It's still raining and there's not much fun in going out in it, so we might as well solve the mystery now."

"Ha! Ha!" said Dickie.

Then Peter made a sensible suggestion.

"I've been wondering whether John Smith has ganged up with Jem *because* he's seen the message too. There were three dirty cups on the table and Mrs Clark said that she didn't know what *they* would say if they found out that I'd seen those bits of paper. Now it seems to me that John wanted to meet people who have known the hills round here for a long time. It's something that happened years ago that is important to him. Perhaps 'not scarlet but gold' will only mean something to the older people? Perhaps we ought to ask all the grown-ups we know round here whether the clue means anything to them? I'm sure Mrs Clark thought it was important – and maybe that's why those two are taking her away from her cottage."

"You mean because they're afraid she'll talk?" David suggested. "That makes sense, so perhaps the first thing we ought to do is to try and find her."

"Or sleuth the other two," Dickie said. "We shall only want six whacking great motorbikes and we can follow 'em anywhere! I wish it would stop raining because there's a lot to do."

Then, suddenly as the storm had broken, the clouds cleared and the sun shone. The puddles in the farmyard steamed and, when the Lone Piners went outside, a

THE CAVE

rainbow was spanning the wood and Jenny had an idea.

"I'm going to ask my dad about the clue. He's always lived in Barton and he knows everything about the place. I expect Peter and David have got a lot to talk about, so the twins and Harry can come down to the village with me. We'll take Mackie and you two can have a nice cosy talk and be thinking about the clue. If you go out, please leave a message with Trudie."

It was raining again by the time Jenny led them proudly into Barton's only general store. The bell above the door jangled and Mr Harman, in a bright blue sweater, appeared almost as if by magic, in the gloom at the back of the shop. He smiled affectionately at his daughter and shook hands with the twins.

Harriet shook hands too, and Mr Harman said he was pleased to meet her and asked them all to stay to tea if Mrs Harman didn't mind.

During the meal Jenny tried the clue on her father and stepmother, but the words meant nothing to them.

"Sounds a bit like the name of a pub but not quite," Mr Harman said. "You're not trying to play a trick on us, are you? 'Not scarlet but gold' sounds daft to me and I've never heard it before."

It was when they were downstairs in the shop again, and Jenny was showing them all sorts of treasures, that Dickie asked Mr Harman the question to which they got such an important reply.

"And have you been selling anything extra special and exciting today, sir?"

"It's strange that you should ask that, my boy, because I've had an unusual customer this very morning, and some very odd things he bought too. Lucky for him, and for me, that I had everything he wanted . . . Didn't you tell me, Jen, that you had a pleasant-looking young fellow in the other day wanting a room in the village?"

"Yes, Dad. Good-looking and brown, with white teeth and wearing leather shorts. Was your special customer like that?"

Mr Harman didn't realise that they were all hanging on his words. "That's right, Jen. Might well be the same bloke. Rather a peculiar way of speaking but he knew what he wanted."

"What did he want?" Jenny asked, casually.

"Might have been setting up house," her father went on. "He bought pounds of tinned stuff, all the candles we've got . . . And that reminds me, I must order more. Doesn't do to be out of candles. Just remind me, Jen."

"Yes, Dad. I'll remind you. What else did he buy?"

"You remember that electric lantern, Jen? The one with a spot of rust on it? He bought that and never said a word about the rust, and bought three spare batteries. You'll never guess what he asked for next, Jen."

"No, Dad. I couldn't guess. What else did he buy?"

"Rope. All I'd got. Clothes lines really, but I sold him two hanks. Over £50 he spent, easy as kiss your hand."

"Fantastic, Dad. Today's your lucky day. But we must be going now. Thank Mum again for the tea. Don't worry about us. We're having a great time at Seven Gates and all we want is fine weather. Tom's coming over soon, I hope."

As soon as they had said goodbye and were all outside, Jenny looked carefully up and down the street.

"Our lucky day too," she whispered. "That must have been John Smith, and do you know why he was buying candles, torches and rope and all that food, Harry?"

"I don't suppose she could know," Mary broke in. "But we do. John Smith has bought all those things, 'cos he's going to one of the caves or old mines, like the one we know between Greystone and Black Dingles. I suppose Jem has told him about them and that's where he's going to hide in case Charles sends the police after him. What are we going to do?"

Jenny looked up at the sky. The clouds were rolling up again from the west and the daylight was fading. She knew that they ought to go back to Seven Gates, but here was a wonderful opportunity for her to impress Harriet and to lead an expedition in the absence of David or Peter.

"I'll tell you," she said breathlessly. "We'll all go up Greystone Dingle and show Harry the cave we found ages ago. We've got Mackie with us and we shall have to be very careful, but that cave is the sort of place that Jem might know. Suppose that's where he's taken John Smith? Suppose we could spy on them and go back and tell Peter and David what we've discovered? You'll come, won't you Harry?"

"Of course I will . . . But what will we do if they *are* there and catch us?"

Jenny didn't want to face this possibility so she ignored it. "Even if they are in there, they'll never catch *us*. We've been in that secret place before and we can crawl in very quietly. You twins will come, won't you?"

Dickie answered. "There'll be trouble about us if we're late back. Nag, nag, nag, o' course, but we'll come, won't we Mary?"

His sister nodded. "There's a secret river and a pool in there, Harry, and it's all inside the middle of the mountain and rather ghosty and cold. Somebody told us it's an old mine. Are you scared to come, Harry?"

"Yes, I am," Harriet gulped. "But I want to go all the same. You didn't say anything to me about this place when we went up to the Chair this morning. Are you sure it's not too far? It's getting dark."

"We'll show you Greystone, anyway," Jenny said.

"It's much worse than Black Dingle. Come on!"

The entrance to Greystone was through a wood close to the village, and as they walked up the dingle the lower slopes of the Stiperstones were on their right and if they had been able to climb over the mountain they would have come down into Black Dingle and been close to Seven Gates. Greystone Dingle made many twists and turns and the higher they climbed the more desolate and forbidding were the steep slopes on each side of the track. This dingle, indeed, was rather like a railway cutting, but the sides were screes of loose stones and as the Lone Piners toiled up the track they could hear the trickle of water and the rattle of falling debris. Harriet had never seen such a desolate, eerie place, for there was no grass on the screes and all that seemed to grow in this grim valley were a few hawthorns and hollies on the upper slopes.

The twins walked ahead with Mackie trotting disconsolately at their heels. Even *they* seemed to be affected by the gloom of the place and had little to say to each other. Jenny, to keep her courage up, chattered vaguely about their previous adventures, but it was Harriet, the new member, who was the first to see the deep imprint of a motorbike's tyres in a muddy patch on the track. This was a real clue, and as they all stood round looking at it Jenny wondered – although she didn't say so – whether they should not go back to Seven Gates and tell the others of their discovery. It was unlikely that anyone other than Jem would ride a motorbike up this slippery and dangerous track on such a day. And he wouldn't have come up here unless he was going to hide in the old mine, because this path led only up to the Devil's Chair. Jenny looked round at the others, wishing that Tom was with them. She did not want to make a decision herself.

THE CAVE

Mary took Mackie's lead from her pocket and clipped it on his collar.

"We'll go first if you like, Jenny. If they're in there, they won't expect us, and we'll hear them before they hear us. Just as soon as we're sure, we'll get out quick as we can and run all the way back to Seven Gates . . . Come on. Let's get it over quickly."

Jenny had no choice now but to lead, but every step she took up the rough track increased her foreboding. The clouds were so low that the Devil's Chair was once again hidden. The steep sides of the dingle closed in on them and the only sound, besides the crunch of their footsteps, was the whisper of the little streams running down the loose shale. Ten minutes later, when it was nearly dark, Jenny left the track and scrambled up to a little rocky plateau.

"We must tell Harry now what it's like inside," she whispered. "It will be too dark to see anything, and we mustn't talk, because if those two are hiding in there they may hear us. All we want to know for certain is that they *are* there . . . I'll go first, then Mary with Mackie, then Harry and Dickie at the back. We must all hold on to each other . . . Now, Harry. The entrance to the cave is behind that big rock. There's a sandy passage which leads to one of the entrances of the old mine that we've never explored properly, and then we go downhill to the left, where there's a pool fed by a stream. I expect we'll hear the waterfall because there's been a lot of rain. There are lots of places to camp out and hide, beyond the pool, and lots more caves and passages which are dangerous. Don't forget that we must keep quiet once we're in there."

Harriet gulped and hoped that the others couldn't hear the thudding of her heart.

Mary said, "S'pose they're in there and come after

us. What shall we do in the dark?"

"Get out quickly, of course," her twin muttered.

Harriet whispered, "Where do you think Jem has hidden his motorbike if he's gone into the cave? Would it be more sensible to find that first?"

"He could leave it higher up the track, but it's not worth looking for it now," Jenny replied. "There are places behind the rocks just up there. He couldn't get it up this slope into the cave, anyway. We'll just have a quick look round inside and then get back."

But it didn't work out like that.

Mary whispered words of comfort to Macbeth, who was whining with excitement, looped the dog's lead round her wrist and then took Jenny's hand. Then in single file they squeezed by the rock and into the entrance of the mine. The sand was soft underfoot and it was very dark. Jenny, with one hand against the damp wall, led them up the slope until she came to the junction of another passage on the left. As she entered this she heard the distant murmur of water. They went carefully twenty yards down a slope, turned another corner and saw the glimmer of a light.

Jenny stopped. The noise of falling water was loud enough now to cover the sound of their whispering as they huddled together.

"This passage leads to a ledge of rock above the pool," Jenny whispered to Harriet. "There's a sort of beach just below when the pool isn't too full. Remember, Mary?"

"Yes, I do. Perhaps those two are setting up a camp? We must go closer and make sure. If they're down by the water, we could hide on the ledge and listen. Would you like us twins to go on alone and spy out the land? I couldn't be more frightened than I am this very minute."

"Let's all go," Harriet said. "We must stick together... I can hear music now."

"I bet Jem has got a transistor," Jenny said. "I bet when he's not on his bike he carries a transistor round in his hand and plays it all the time. Come on."

When they reached the ledge above the pool Jenny lay down on the cold rock and crawled forward until she could look down over the edge. The others followed.

Jem Clark and John Smith were sitting on the beach with their backs to the rocks. Three candles guttered beside them and the light of a big electric lamp shone on a map across John's knees. The sound of the waterfall at the end of the cave and the murmur from the radio drowned their voices, even though the Lone Piners were only a few feet above them. Suddenly John leaned across and switched off the transistor, and at once they could hear what he was saying.

Later Jenny confessed that, although they could not have been listening for more than five minutes, the time before they were discovered seemed like an hour. The four of them were so spellbound by what they heard that they forgot Macbeth who, crouching by Mary, soon lost his patience. Suddenly he jumped forward to the edge of the ledge and began to bark furiously. With a curse John Smith swung the beam of the big spotlight up towards them, while Jem jumped to his feet and knocked over one of the candles.

Harriet screamed as Mackie, in his excitement and fury, disappeared over the edge. Mary, with the loop of his lead still round her wrist, struggled to haul him back and then, realising that she was half-strangling the little dog as he dangled above the two men, she decided to follow him and jump.

She landed on hands and knees on the outspread map and then grabbed the snarling Mackie and got up.

Jem swore monotonously as usual.

"It's those kids again! Now we've got 'em here they'd better stay."

"Shut up," John replied as he flashed the light into Mary's eyes. "You're one of those kids from Seven Gates, aren't you? How long have you been here?"

Mary, realising that none of her friends had yet given themselves away, called up all her courage.

"Oh, dear!" she said, as calmly as she could. "What an excitement! I do hope I didn't frighten you? It's my little dog, you see. He must have recognised you . . . Dickie! Can you see who I've found? It's that nice man John Smith who is Peter's friend. He came to see us at Seven Gates last night . . . How do you do again, Mr Smith? Fancy seeing you in our cave. Acksherley, the cave really belongs to us. We found it ages ago, but I s'pose we don't mind you sitting in it."

Here she paused for breath, and then John said, "Stop talking and listen. Is Peter up there too? Where is your brother?"

Mary backed against the rock, turned quickly and held up the struggling Macbeth after slipping his lead from her wrist.

"Take Mackie, please, twin. I can't think why our dog doesn't like you, John. You don't mind if I call you John, do you? . . . Oh! You mean my *big* brother, David. I hope he's waiting outside for us with Peter."

Mackie, still barking defiance, was now safely on the ledge again, and in the light of the flickering candles Mary saw that the face of the rock had several wide cracks running across it.

"Help me up!" she shouted to the others, and began to scramble up. Jenny, leaning over as far as she dared, grasped her wrists and took her weight as Jem grabbed her ankle. Mary kicked him in the face with her free

THE CAVE

foot, and sobbed with relief as he cursed and let go. Then Dickie, shouting "Up the Lone Piners!" with Jenny's help hauled her up to the ledge.

Harriet, who had been holding Jenny so that she would not be pulled over, gave Mary a quick hug. The beam of John's spotlight swung up again and picked out the four of them backing into the gallery. He shouted something they couldn't hear as they stumbled up the slope towards freedom. Again and again Jenny blundered into the wall of the passage, and once she tripped over Macbeth and fell full length. They reached the turning and stumbled into the passage that led down to the entrance.

At last they struggled, sobbing with relief and the pain of their bruises and grazes, out on to the little plateau. There wasn't much of a moon, but it was not as dark between the grim slopes of the dingle as it had been inside the mountain.

"You were *brave*, Mary," Jenny gasped. "So brave."

Mary clung to her hand. "I'm frightened *now*. Let's run. Jem might come after us on his bike . . . Let Mackie off his lead now, twin. Poor little darling, he was the bravest of us all, really."

The track down the dingle was under water in some places, for the little streams whispering down through the shale were bigger now. They all ran until Harriet was doubled up with stitch and then they trotted. Down the sinister dingle they hurried, listening for the sound of pursuing footsteps or the dreaded roar of a motorcycle engine. After ten minutes, Jenny saw the gleam of a wavering light ahead. She stopped, with a hand to her mouth, when the others came up to her.

"It's true," she whispered. "I've always tried to pretend that the Stiperstones aren't haunted, but they are. I've heard tell that a light like that could be the ghost of Wild Edric who rides the hills before

101

something awful happens. I'm scared."

"I don't think it's Edric," Dickie said. "Look at Mackie."

The moon, clear for a moment of the scudding clouds, showed them the little dog standing on the track with his head on one side and one paw lifted. His tail was moving gently.

Dickie put his fingers to his mouth and whistled the Lone Piners' secret call to each other, the peewit's plaintive cry.

The answer came back and the light moved quickly towards them.

"I think it's David," Mary sighed. "I don't think we're going to like what he says to us."

They didn't like it at all. None of them had ever known him so angry, and as they knew they were in the wrong there wasn't much they could say when he accused them of being thoughtless and stupid. Jenny took the blame, but Harriet interrupted her.

"All right, David. We're sorry, but can't you see that we've had enough? You should thank us instead of grumbling, because we've found Jem and John and we know they're looking for money that was hidden somewhere round here by German spies in the war. John's father was a spy and John has come over from Germany to find what he left in these hills. He's making Jem help him, but we don't know what they've done with Mrs Clark and they don't know what 'Not scarlet but gold' means any more than we do. We heard them talking before they knew we were there."

"And now you can shut up bullying us," Dickie added. "Mary has been very brave, but we're utterly worn out solving all these mysteries and if Peter was here she'd understand. And this is one of the times when we utterly loathe you."

CHAPTER 9

Jenny Alone

When Jenny woke up next morning, the sun was shining through the dusty window of the granary. She sat up in her sleeping-bag and realised that her body was aching all over. Then she remembered last night's adventure inside the mountain and the panicky race down the narrow track of the dingle.

She wondered what the time was. Harriet and Mary were still asleep and there was no sign of Peter except the agreeable smell of frying bacon wafting up from below. Jenny didn't want to talk to Peter alone because she too had been very scathing last night, so it seemed a good idea to wake the other two girls.

"Get dressed quickly so that we're ready before they shout for us," Jenny hissed. "We'll go down together and then we'll have to decide what we're going to do now that we know what Jem and John are after. We shall have to make David and Peter realise that we were all very brave and clever – especially Mary, of course."

Mary pulled her blue sweater over her head and grinned.

"Don't you worry, Jenny. We won't let David bully you again. He was mad last night because they didn't think about the cave themselves. The only thing I'm worried about is whether Charles and Trudie know about our adventures. We shall have to get Peter on our side anyway... Are you listening to us, Harry?"

Harriet crawled out of her bag and blinked at them.

"Of course I am. I do hope there isn't going to be an awful row with the others. I hate quarrels and everything seems to be going wrong with this holiday."

"Not *everything,*" Jenny said. "It's stopped raining,

the sun is shining and, after all, whatever David and Peter say we *did* have an adventure and we *have* found where Jem and John Smith are hiding."

"*Were* hiding," Harriet said as she began to dress. "I bet they won't be there for long, now that we know where they are. Why don't we forget all about them and just enjoy ourselves today?"

Before either of them could answer this sensible question, Peter called from below.

"Come and get your breakfast, you lazy lot. I've been doing all the work this morning, but *you'll* have to wash up."

David was pouring out the tea when the three girls came down and he didn't look up.

"Oh, dear," Mary said. "He's cross again. All the same, David dear, we do thank you very much, and please where is my twin and where is my Mackie?"

Peter forked two rashers of bacon and a slice of fried bread on to a plate and passed it across.

"Your twin," she said, "is what you would describe as being sunk in swinish slumber. I brought Mackie down when you were all sunk in the same thing, and when I last saw him he was scratching himself in the farmyard."

David, glancing across at Dickie's "dormitory," shouted, "RICHARD, you lazy little so-and-so, GET UP! Your twin is eating your breakfast."

A muffled cry came from the shadows at the far end of the barn as Dickie rushed out of his cubicle.

"You beasts! You deliberately let me sleep on. I was dreaming I smelt bacon."

Dickie treated Peter to one of his dazzling smiles as he grabbed a plate of bacon. Then he sat down next to Jenny.

For a few minutes they all ate in a silence which was eventually broken by Harriet.

"Well," she said brightly. "What are we all going to do today? I was saying upstairs that I hoped we could forget all about Jem and John Smith now that we've found out where they're hiding, although we don't think they'll stay there now that we *do* know."

David looked across meaningly at Peter and then asked Jenny to tell them again everything that had happened.

Jenny repeated everything they had overheard.

"And I am sorry you didn't know where we were and that you had to come and look for us. I know we ought to have come back and told you two about what Dad said, and about the track of Jem's motorbike, but we just wanted to find out all we could – and sort of surprise you."

"Don't worry," David said grimly. "You managed to do that. I wouldn't have believed you could all be so stupid. You're not safe to let out alone . . . Are you sure that John said that his father was a German spy in the last war?"

And from there they began to argue it all over again. After a while David admitted that Charles and Trudie did not know of last night's adventure and that there didn't seem to be any particular reason why they should be told now that John and Jem had established themselves in the cave.

"But if it's true that John is searching for money or something which his father hid in these hills in the war," Peter said eagerly, "surely we have as much right as anybody to search for it too? If we found it, I can't see that we should be stealing. Of course, we should have to tell the police or somebody, but we know about 'not scarlet but gold,' and as we also know all this countryside we've just got to start thinking and trying to work it out. It's like a puzzle. It sounds like a crossword clue and I don't see why we shouldn't try and solve it while we're here."

The others looked at her in surprise, for this speech was much more like the old Peter whom they hadn't seen much of since they had arrived at Seven Gates.

David laughed. "Fair enough, but those two are dangerous and we've all got to keep out of their way... Are you absolutely sure, Jenny, that John said that his father would have left money?"

"Of course we're sure," Jenny snapped. "We all heard him. He was explaining to Jem that he had come specially from Germany to try and find it, but I'm certain, as Peter says, that we share the only clue he's got."

Harriet suggested – but without much hope – that they should not waste their time looking for something which certainly didn't belong to them even if it had ever existed.

But Peter was keen to go on and, even if the others were surprised, David knew very well that she was still angry with herself for being taken in by John's charm.

"We're fed up with all this talk, talk and nag, nag," Dickie said suddenly. "My twin and I know that we've got to find this treasure before the enemy. It's the only thing to do. If Jem and John are so keen to find it, then they must be sure about it... Come on, Mary. Let's go by ourselves if no one else wants to come."

David and Peter and the others followed the twins into the farmyard, and they all sat on the top bar of the gate across the track which led down through the pine-wood. David took control.

"Let's check up on what we know," he said, "and then let's try and imagine what we would do if we were John and Jem. They're looking for money which John's father must have hidden in the Stiperstones. Jenny says that John admitted to Jem that he had been given a letter written by his father years ago, saying that if he didn't come back to Germany it would mean that he was dead and that there would be a chance of his son finding the money. It's a bit far-fetched, but I suppose it's possible. Peter believes that Mrs Clark might have befriended John's father. Perhaps she gave him shelter when he was on the run, and 'not scarlet but gold' is the only clue he left with her."

"Why didn't she follow it up before then?" Jenny asked. "She's always been poor and I should think she could have done with the money."

"Perhaps she didn't realise it was a clue," Peter replied. "I think she'd only just unpicked that patchwork quilt. Perhaps John and Jem made her do that. I wish we knew where Mrs Clark is. If we could find her, she might tell us more, but I'm sure she spoils Jem and he doesn't care about her. She'll do anything he tells her, I believe. He's horrible. They wouldn't dare hide her in the cave, would they?"

None of the others thought that possible.

David said firmly, "I know what we've got to do. We must have maps of the district, like the ones John was looking at in the cave. We'll have to work on those just as they were doing. We've got to look at every inch and check the name of every farm and stream and hill and see whether anything gives us a clue to 'not scarlet but gold.' I'm a fool because I didn't bring our maps this time. There may be one locked up in Witchend, but the quickest way will be for some of us to go into Shrewsbury and get them. We shall want two large-scale maps because we must cover the Long Mynd as well. Why don't you lot take Harriet and show her the town? You can get a bus from Barton."

"So we can," Jenny agreed unenthusiastically, "but what are *you* going to do? And what about Peter? Why don't you come with us, Peter?"

Peter looked quizzically at David.

"Thank you, Jenny, but I've got to keep an eye on David."

"You might as well go with the others, Peter," the latter said. "There's something I want to do while we're waiting for the maps. You'll be back this afternoon, anyway."

"Don't be silly, David. We all know you're going to explore the cave and see whether those two are still there. I'm coming too, so it's no good putting on a strong-man act."

David tried to argue with her, but when they walked away together it was Mary who suggested they go off to Shrewsbury at once.

Dickie agreed. "And we'll have a meal out. It will be rather sumptuous to have a meal we don't have to wash up."

Harriet looked at him in astonishment. "Honestly, Dickie, you get better and better. I like your vocab. Let's go! I suppose we take Mackie. Is he good in buses?"

Mary spoke with cold disdain.

"My darling goes wherever I go. He's wonderful in buses and carries his ticket in his collar."

So they went to Shrewsbury. Jenny knew everybody on the bus, but few of the passengers had seen the twins before and this was a situation much appreciated by Dickie and Mary. The farther they got away from Seven Gates and the Stiperstones, the more cheerful they became.

"Good morning one and all and hail to you," Dickie said as he led the way to an empty double seat at the back of the bus, while Mary, with Macbeth in her arms, treated the passengers to a ravishing smile. Harriet was a little embarrassed, particularly when the rather dour-looking man next to whom she was sitting remarked, "Staying with that crowd up at Seven Gates, I reckon?"

Harriet, a Londoner, could never understand how country people managed to know so much about their neighbours, but she just said, "Yes. We reckon we are at Seven Gates and we like it very much."

The conductor who was regarding Macbeth with suspicion, was sure that he had never transported twins, who looked exactly alike, on his bus before. He felt that something unusual was about to happen.

"Please may I ask you *not* to look at my dog as if you didn't like him," Mary suggested politely. "He wants to go to Shrewsbury and has asked me to buy his ticket for him, but he gets upset if people don't like him."

"He'll get upset off my bus then – and I don't want no cheek. If I don't like dogs on my bus, then off they go."

"Jenny!" Mary gasped. "You know this man and you let him talk like that to us! Tell him we're not allowed to be upset, either. Tell him we've come to be with you at Seven Gates because we've been very, very ill for a very long time and the doctor says that twins like us mustn't be upset."

"Acksherley," Dickie broke in cheerfully, "when we're upset we get sick, which is very unlucky for us ... I'm not feeling very well now," and he rolled up his eyes and leaned back in his seat.

Harriet looked horrified, but Jenny saved the situation by informing the passengers that the twins were only showing off. And so the time passed quickly and it did not seem long before they got out at the Shrewsbury bus station. Mackie had never liked crowds, and as it was market day the pavements were thronged. They bought the two maps without difficulty and then Dickie suggested food at his favourite café.

The meal was good, and as they were early they got a table in the window in the upstairs room from which they could watch the crowds below. The café was opposite a big store and they had just finished double strawberry ice-creams when Harriet suggested that they might show her the Stiperstones map, and see if they could discover anything which would help them to solve the riddle of "not scarlet but gold". While Dickie was struggling to unfold it, Jenny glanced down into the street. On the opposite pavement a shabbily dressed woman seemed to be looking straight up at them. Jenny's heart thumped with the sudden shock as she realised that she was staring down at Mrs Clark. So Jem's mother hadn't gone very far after all, and now, without a doubt, was a chance to follow her and see if she was staying in Shrewsbury.

"Mrs Clark is down there and I'm going to follow her. Pay the bill, Harry, and we'll meet at the café at the bus station in an hour . . . Nobody else is to come, please. I know her and can keep out of her way, but she might be suspicious of lots of us . . . *Please, Harry, don't argue.* Look after the twins, I won't be long, I promise," and before any of them could protest Jenny was running down the stairs. Mrs Clark was now looking into the window of the store. Two buses passed slowly and Jenny lost sight of her, and by the time she was able to cross the road Mrs Clark had disappeared. In desperation Jenny looked up at the window of the café and saw Dickie grimacing and pointing to the shop.

Jenny pushed back the swing doors. The store was enormous and the counters stretched away into the dim distance. Jenny tried to think what Mrs Clark would want to buy, but she couldn't be sure whether the woman had recognised her. Probably not. There was no reason why she should remember her, and even if she did it was not unusual for Jenny to be in Shrewsbury. She often was.

So Jenny pushed past toothbrushes and strong-smelling soaps and toilet articles, and then she saw Mrs Clark a few yards away, by the stationery counter. She was buying a writing pad and a ball-point pen and she looked frightened and unhappy and after she had made her purchase she walked through the store and out into the street again by another door.

Jenny followed, certain now that the woman's glance up at the windows of the café had been innocent enough.

It was easy enough for Jenny to keep out of sight in the shopping crowds, but not so easy when Mrs Clark turned off into the side streets where there were not so many people. Once Jenny nearly lost her, for the woman turned a corner suddenly when she was about thirty yards ahead. As Jenny ran to the corner, a man stepped suddenly on to the pavement from a house and she bumped into him.

After mumbling that she was sorry, she took to her heels and raced for the corner round which Mrs Clark had disappeared.

She turned the corner into another narrow street, which was empty but for two cats in the gutter. Mrs Clark was not there. It was a long street and, as she couldn't possibly have reached the end in the time, she must have gone into a house. Jenny was in despair. After all her fine talk and ideas, she had failed.

She was halfway down the street when Mrs Clark suddenly came out of a newsagent's shop about forty yards ahead. There was nowhere for Jenny to hide, so she stopped short, stooped, and retied her shoe-lace. She was sure Mrs Clark was staring at her and prayed that she would not recognise her red head or her green anorak or realise that she was being followed. Cautiously Jenny looked up and was thankful to see that the woman was walking ahead again without a backward glance.

The next alarm came a few minutes later when a motorbike roared down the narrow street behind Jenny. Mrs Clark heard it too, stopped and turned round.

There was nothing Jenny could do now, for there was not even a shop between her and Mrs Clark. To retie her shoe-lace again would surely give the game away and, in sudden panic, she realised that the woman thought that the motorcyclist might be Jem.

Jenny walked on as slowly as she could, and when the

bike had passed her she crossed the road. It was impossible to recognise the rider, but he roared past Mrs Clark as well, so presumably he was a stranger. A minute later the woman turned again to the left, without looking behind her, while Jenny, now feeling shaken but almost reckless, followed and stopped at the corner. She was in time to see Mrs Clark opening the door of a house opposite the first lamp-post on the left-hand pavement.

So this looked like the end of the journey. Once Jenny had checked the number of the house she could go back to the bus station and tell the others of her discovery, and they would then decide whether to return to Seven Gates at once and report to David and Peter, or take some action on their own.

Jenny sighed thankfully. The palms of her hands were damp and her heart was banging uncomfortably. Then she looked up at the name of the street. Bedford Avenue was rather a grand name for so shabby a road. There wasn't a tree in sight and all the houses looked alike except that some needed a fresh coat of paint more than others. They were built in pairs and in front of each was a low iron fence and gate, and between the fence and each house was a patch of ground which might once have been called a garden. It was a sad street of lost hopes.

Jenny though quickly. She knew that once again she had been impulsive rather than brave because she wanted to impress Harriet and the twins. She was also rather sore with David and Peter because, although she wanted their romance to prosper, she resented the way in which they had sent her off with the twins and Harriet. They seemed to forget that she was fifteen now, and she still felt that they hadn't appreciated the discovery of Jem's and John's hiding place. Of course there was danger in the dark mine last night, but now it was daylight and there was no reason to suspect that Jem was with his mother. Then Jenny remembered how Peter had told them that Mrs Clark had admitted that "they" were making her go away and leave her home. And last night, crouching on the rocky ledge above Jem and John as they discussed their plans, it had been obvious that both of them cared nothing for Mrs Clark. They wanted her kept out of the way while they searched for the treasure, and Jenny was fairly sure that if they were successful, Mrs Clark's share wouldn't amount to much.

And so Jenny was suddenly sure that Mrs Clark was not only a frightened and unhappy woman, but that she might not even know where her son was or what he was doing.

This, then, was Jenny's chance. There would be little or no danger in daylight and there was plenty of time to get back to the bus station before the others arrived: so, without a backward glance, she ran down Bedford Avenue and stopped beside the first lamp-post.

Number thirty-nine was like all the other houses, except that the "front garden" was a patch of concrete with dandelions growing in the cracks. The iron gate was half open and, before her courage went, Jenny pushed the gate back and knocked on the door. She knocked firmly, twice, and then stepped back and looked at the window of the front room. The curtains of yellow lace moved and Jenny was sure she was being watched.

She took a deep breath and knocked again. The door opened suddenly and there was Mrs Clark staring at her with piercing black eyes. She was wearing a shabby black dress and a red cardigan. She had taken off her coat and hat, and Jenny could see the wide streak of white across her hair. She was also instantly aware that Mrs Clark was frightened.

"Go away," the woman whispered. "Go away! How

dare you make such a noise with your knocking!"

Jenny stepped into the hall and closed the door. The smell of the house was horrid – stale cooking.

"You're Mrs Clark," she said breathlessly. "I know you. I'm Jenny Harman and I live in Barton Beach. I want to talk to you. Are you alone here?"

"Get out! Get out! I don't know what you mean. I'm not Mrs Clark. I'll call somebody if you don't go."

"You *are* Mrs Clark. I know you are. I followed you through the town because we – that's my friends at Seven Gates – are sure we can help you. We know all sorts of things like 'not scarlet but gold,' and we know–"

Mrs Clark grabbed her shoulder so hard that Jenny cried out with pain, then pushed her into the front room and closed the door behind her.

"So you're one of them prying, nosy kids, are you? Harman, eh? Maybe I remember you and maybe you've made a big mistake following me. If *he* knew, I don't know what he'd do to you – or to me for that matter."

Jenny shook herself free and looked round the room. Along one wall was a bed covered with a patchwork quilt. There was a small table with a plant on it in the window and a bigger table covered with sheets of newspaper in the centre of the room. On this table was half a loaf, a pot of marmalade, a teapot and cup and saucer, and the writing pad and ball-point pen which Jenny had seen Mrs Clark buy in the town. The grate was full of ashes. On one side of the fireplace was a tall cupboard and on the other, a big, old-fashioned wardrobe. There were also two straight-backed chairs.

Jenny backed to the fireplace, thought of Tom and held her chin high. She was still sure that she was not as frightened as Mrs Clark.

"We know that you didn't want to leave your cottage, Mrs Clark. We know that Jem is in trouble about the fire at the farm and we know that he's hiding with John Smith. We're sure you can help us and we know that we can help you too. We've often helped people. You're afraid, aren't you? Are you living here alone? We know where Jem is."

Mrs Clark gave a cry and put her hand to her mouth.

"You don't. You couldn't know. I don't know. You're a little liar. You're crazy too. There's nobody in this house but us. This is my sister's house and she's out for the day and I'm staying here for a holiday and before you go you'll tell me a few things ... Come here."

But Jenny didn't move, for even while the woman was speaking she heard the roar of a high-powered motorcycle. Nearer and nearer it came in a crescendo of sound and suddenly there was a shadow against the window curtains as the bike stopped outside Number Thirty-nine. The engine was still pop-popping as the helmeted rider got off.

"It's Jem," Mrs Clark whispered. "He's come back. If he catches you here, I don't know what he'll do. Get in that wardrobe and keep quiet. *Get in, you little fool.* You don't know what he's like when he's angry."

She opened the big wardrobe in the corner, pushed Jenny in against a soft barrier of clinging clothes and closed the door. Jenny struggled to turn round and face the thin cracks of light which showed where the door didn't quite fit. She fought against panic in the hot, stuffy darkness and pressed her face against the crack by the latch for more air.

She heard the slam of the front door, footsteps in the hall and then Jem's hard, cruel voice.

"Lucky I've found you in. Where's Aunt Elsie?"

"You gave me quite a shock, Jem. I wish you'd let me know when you're coming. Elsie is out for the day. Would you like a nice cup o' tea?"

"I would not. I've got no time to waste, Mum, but I want money. Now. You've got some put away somewhere I know, and I've got to have a hundred quid right away. Things aren't going too well and I'm in a bit of trouble."

"Oh dear, Jem. You're such a worry to me. I haven't got enough money to give you any. I've only enough for my food and things while I'm staying here, and I'll tell you right now, Jem, that I won't ask my sister Elsie for a penny. Why should I? She's no money to spare and times are hard for her ... Come in the kitchen, Jem, and I'll make you a nice cup o' tea. It's more cosy in there."

Jenny knew then that Mrs Clark was trying to get Jem out of the room so that she could escape. Obviously Mrs Clark wouldn't want her to overhear this conversation. But Jem didn't want tea. He just wanted his own way as usual – and quickly.

Jenny couldn't see, but she guessed that he had taken off his crash helmet and was now sitting at the table. There was a moment or two's silence and then she smelled cigarette smoke. Only a faint whiff came through the crack, but it made Jenny feel sick. She was fighting for breath now and perspiration was trickling down her face. She clenched her hands and prayed that she wouldn't faint as Jem began to speak again.

"Now listen, Mum, because I've not much time. I've got to have money and I know you've got some hid away."

"I haven't, son. It's in the cottage. In a safe place."

"Tell me where and I'll get it."

"I won't say, Jem. I've done everything for you, but that's all I've got. You durstn't go back to the cottage anyway. They're looking for you."

"Will you give me the money if I clear off and never come back? That's what I want it for, Mum. They're after me and I've made up my mind they'll never catch me ... *What's that noise?*"

The noise was Jenny's head falling against the wardrobe door. She struggled again to hold it up as Mrs Clark raised her voice in reply.

"There's no noise, lad."

"Tell me where the money is. Just give me fifty quid now and I'll clear out."

"You've said that before. And what about John Smith? Where's he? He's got plenty of money."

"That's what I wanted to tell you about Mum," Jem began, and then his voice rose hysterically as he begged his mother to help him find the money hidden by Schmidt nearly twenty years ago. Just as John had done, he tried to force his mother to remember anything that would help him now to discover the treasure. He made her wild promises. He said she could live anywhere she liked. Should go for a long holiday. Should have electric light in the cottage if she preferred to stay there. Then he showed his true colours and said he no longer cared what happened to John Smith and that he was going to give his share of the money to his mother. All he asked was that she should *make* herself remember the meaning or the reason of "not scarlet but gold," which she had thought so important to remember that she had sewed the words into the patchwork.

Then he saw the quilt on the bed by the wall and his voice rose excitedly.

"There's another! Did you make that? Give me a knife. Cut it up. See if there's anything else there."

"No, no, Jem! That's Elsie's. She showed me how to make quilts years ago . . . I can't go on with this, Jem. I've had enough. I've tried and tried to remember something I want to forget. I can't remember any more. *I don't believe he ever hid anything. I don't believe there is any money.* You're wasting your time."

Inside the wardrobe Jenny felt her knees giving way.

Everything was whirling round and round and there were bright lights like coloured stars before her eyes. Dimly, from far away, she heard the hated voice of Jem say, "You silly old fool. I'll *make* you remember. We've been too soft with you."

Then Jenny's hands beat against the wardrobe door, which burst open as she slumped against it, and she fell in a heap of old clothing on to the floor.

In the long silence that followed, while she gulped air into her lungs, she could actually hear footsteps in the street. Then, still fighting for breath, she got to her knees and looked up. When she saw the hatred in Jem's eyes and the look he gave his mother, Jenny was sure that she had never been so frightened in her life.

CHAPTER 10

Enter Tom

The twins and Harriet, watching from the café, saw Mrs Clark turn and look into the window of the store. They could not see Jenny until she had crossed the road after the two buses had passed, but they did see Mrs Clark go into the shop. As soon as Dickie had signalled Jenny to follow her, he nodded to Mary and began to fold up the map he had been showing to Harriet.

"Please pay the bill, Harry," he said. "We mustn't let Jenny know we're following her; it won't be easy because there's three of us and Mackie, but we must try."

"But we can't do that," Harriet protested. "Jenny told me to look after you two and we can't *all* follow Mrs Clark."

"We're following *Jenny*," Mary explained patiently as she got up. "We can't just let her go off like that, exposed to fearful perils. You know very well, Harry, that's not the sort of thing Lone Piners do . . . There are two doors to that shop and one of them is farther down the street. I'll watch that one with Mackie, from the opposite pavement. Dickie will spy out the land from below here and you watch from the window until you've paid the bill . . . Come on, Mackie! We're on the trail again and you must protect your loved ones."

By the time Harriet had found her purse the twins had clattered down the stairs. She had to wait a few minutes for the bill, and it wasn't until she was in the street that she realised that the twins had not said they would wait for her if they picked up Jenny's trail in the meantime. She needn't have worried, because the café door had barely closed behind her when Dickie, who had been standing in the doorway of the next shop, sidled up to her and spoke out of the side of his mouth while looking in the opposite direction.

"You don't know me, sister," he drawled in what he believed to be a cowboy's accent. "Don't look at me, sister. Keep your eyes skinned on that thar door opposite. The old woman ain't come out yet . . Bide where you are, sister, unless you see them two and then call us two. I'm a'joining Mary now," and he sidled along the pavement as if he were carrying a six-shooter on each hip.

Harriet wasn't used to Dickie's sudden excursions into the world of Westerns, but she stayed where she was with her eyes fixed on that thar shop door. Three minutes later Dickie, dodging between the shoppers, came racing back as if he had a football at his toes.

"OK, Harry. Come on. Old Ma Clark is on her way and Jenny is sleuthing her. She didn't see us, but we mustn't get too close."

It was easy to follow Jenny because she never looked round, but Mary suggested that they shouldn't all walk together, so Dickie went first. They all saw Jenny turn sharply to the left into a narrow side street, but before they could follow, Mary suddenly stopped and waved to a cheerful-looking boy on the other side of the street.

"Tom!" she called. "Hi, Tom! It's us!"

Tom Ingles stopped in amazement and then ran across the road to them as Dickie, who had heard his sister's shout, turned back. Tom was sixteen, short but wiry. His black hair was always untidy, his face was always brown because he worked on his uncle's farm by Witchend, and he was the wittiest and most good-humoured of the Lone Piners. He looked at Harriet in surprise, for he had never met her, but before he could say anything Mary clutched his hand and dragged him forward.

"Wonderful seeing you like this, Tom. Honest it is. You must come with us now 'cos we're following Jenny . . . Yes, JENNY. And she's following Mrs Clark who is a sort of enemy but fairly feeble if you know what I mean. *But,* Tom, Mrs Clark has got a son Jem who is a bully and absolutely foul and he's after some treasure left by German spies on the Stiperstones an—"

"STOP IT," Tom shouted. "What are you talking about? And where's Jen and who's this girl?"

"This girl is Harriet Sparrow and she's a Lone Piner as you should know perfectly well," Dickie said.

"Hullo, Harriet," Tom said. "Are you as mad as these kids? I thought you were all at Seven Gates."

"So we are but we're here as well. Don't be so difficult, Tom . . . Mary and me and Harriet are following Jenny who doesn't know we are. *And why are you here anyway?*"

"We're in Shrewsbury for the market. Uncle Alf is after some sheep and I haven't got to meet him for an hour. I reckon he'll let me come over to you all tomorrow . . . OK, OK, I'll come with you now and you can tell me more about this nonsense of German treasure. And you can tell me as we go what Jen thinks she's doing following old women around."

Harriet thought Tom was wonderful. She'd heard about him from the twins, of course, and she knew what Jenny felt about him and wasn't surprised. He smiled at her as they turned into the side street and she blushed as if he could read her thoughts.

Jenny was not in sight, but slouching towards them was an unpleasant-looking man. Mackie hated him and began to bark and Mary pulled him back on the lead.

"I'm *so* sorry about my dog. He's quite harmless really, but he's rather excitable. Please have you seen our redheaded girl friend down this street? I think p'raps she was in a hurry."

The man muttered and grumbled and said he had seen a kid who was in a hurry and had nearly knocked him over. Soon after this encounter they saw Jenny stooping to tie her shoe-lace, and then they recognised Mrs Clark hurrying along the pavement ahead.

"That's them," Harriet hissed. "Jen is still on the trail. We mustn't let her see us yet. If she does, she may come back to us."

"Specially if she sees Tom." Mary grinned. "Let's go back round the corner and then we can dash down after her when we know where they're going."

While Dickie was peering round the corner a big motorbike passed them. They couldn't recognise the driver, but the twins were sure it wasn't Jem, who would surely have stopped when he saw them.

"Why should he stop?" Tom asked. "If *you* don't stop this silly game of hide and seek and explain what's going on round here and what Jen thinks she's doing. I'm going right after her."

"They've both disappeared round another corner," Dickie hissed. "Now we can run. Hope you're in training, Tom. We'll tell you about this terrific adventure soon as we can."

So they raced down another street and followed Jenny until they reached the corner of Bedford Avenue. They were in time to see her walk up to the door of a house opposite the first lamp-post on the left-hand side.

"What's going on here?" Tom demanded as the twins dragged him back. "Jenny's got no business to be following strangers. What's the idea and where are David and Peter? Do they know about this?"

"Not exactly." Mary tried to explain. "But I don't think they'd be surprised, Tom. They sent us to

Shrewsbury to buy some maps, and from the window of a café we saw Mrs Clark – that's the woman Jenny's following – by mistake."

Tom said, "Are you going to tell me, or not, why Jenny is following an old woman about Shrewsbury and going by herself into a scruffy-looking house like that? "

"We would if we had time," Dickie protested. "Don't be bossy, Tom. We don't think Mrs Clark would hurt Jenny, but we don't know who else is in that house."

Tom shrugged his shoulders and stepped round the corner. The others followed him, just as a big motorbike turned into the far end of Bedford Avenue and roared towards them.

"I bet that's Jem," Mary gasped. "Come back, twin. He mustn't see us," and she dragged Harriet and Dickie back out of sight.

They heard the engine of the motorbike cut out.

"If that *was* Jem, we shall have to rescue Jenny, Dickie. Come on. It doesn't matter who sees us now. We can't leave Jenny in that house."

The three of them, with Mackie ahead tugging at his lead, raced up Bedford Avenue and caught up Tom who was just pushing back the rusty iron gate of Number Thirty-nine. The big black bike was at the kerb.

"Wait, Tom," Dickie puffed. "Just a sec, *please*. If this is Jem's bike, let's unscrew the valves of his tyres in case we have to run for it presently!"

Tom nodded and grinned – they had worked this trick before – and in a few seconds the tyres were flat.

"You lot stay here," Tom said. "I'm going in after Jen."

The front door was ajar, so he pushed it back and the others followed him into the gloomy hall. Harriet was not a coward, and although she had already been mixed up in two adventures with the twins she was not yet taking their courage for granted. She had heard and seen Jem Clark last night and knew that if Mary's guess had been right and that it *was* Jem in the house, there was certainly going to be trouble. And although Tom had told them to stay outside, he didn't seem to be surprised that they had followed him. He didn't even look round when they heard Jenny scream, but kicked open the door of the sitting-room.

Harriet never forgot the next five minutes, nor her first sight of that grubby room. Mrs Clark, white-faced and with tears on her cheeks, was cowering in a chair. With her back to an enormous wardrobe, the door of which was open, was Jenny, with her head held high and her red hair flaming. Jem was standing over her, gripping her wrist and trying to twist it behind her back. As Tom kicked the door open, Jenny must have smacked Jem's face with her free hand for, even as he turned, he was swearing at her.

Then Jenny, with a little sob, said, "Tom! Oh, Tom. You've come after all."

Mary stooped and unclipped Macbeth's lead.

"After him, Mackie. Get him."

Without even finding the time or wasting his breath to bark or growl, Macbeth went into battle. Mrs Clark screamed as a black streak hurtled past her and fastened his teeth into one of Jem's boots. Jem turned and, dragging Jenny so that she fell, he kicked Macbeth so that he yelped with surprise and pain.

"Call the dog off, twins, and get out," Tom said quietly, but in a voice shaking with rage: and then to Jem, "Let her go, you dirty bully."

Jem's weak mouth curled into a sneer, but as Jenny, with her bright eyes still fixed on Tom, struggled up from her knees he released her wrist.

For a moment nobody spoke. Mary fell on Macbeth,

dragging him back from Jem, and with Dickie's help clipped on his lead again. Mrs Clark, with her hand to her mouth, was still sobbing. Harriet, with an arm round Mary's shoulder, noticed that Jenny, still with her back to the wardrobe, was watching Tom with a shaky smile. But Tom was standing very still behind the table while Jem fidgeted on the other side.

"Shut up, you!" Tom said. "Your mouth wants washing out." Then, to Jenny, "Has he hurt you?"

She shook her head slowly, but, without speaking, raised her hand so that they could see the red weal round her wrist where he had gripped it.

Tom Ingles was not excitable or demonstrative. Although, because he was nearly seventeen, he sometimes pretended to have little or no time for the Lone Pine Club and its members, the others were never in any doubt about his friendship. When Jenny held up her wrist and he saw the bruise, and when he looked up and saw tears still on her face, he knew that in spite of all her excitable chatter and sometimes silly ways, she was the best and most loyal friend he had ever had in his life and that she always would be. And in those few seconds he really grew up.

Tom was four or five inches shorter than Jem Clark but he was strong for his weight and height. He was now very angry, and although Harriet and the twins were behind him they were frightened when they heard him say, in a voice which didn't sound at all like his, "Listen, Jenny, and do as I say. Come away from that wardrobe and round by the window and then get out of this house. Take the others. Don't argue. Wait for me outside."

Jenny obeyed. Tom didn't turn to watch her but kept his eyes fixed on Jem, whose fingers were still drumming on the table. Then Jem shrugged his shoulders.

"I don't know and don't care who you are, mate, but

you can get out with the other kids. They've no business here and neither have you. This house belongs to my mum, and that redheaded kid was hiding in the wardrobe. Listening she was. Not minding her own business. *Get out. All of you."*

From behind him, in the doorway, Tom heard Jenny say. "Please come too, Tom. There's nothing else we can do now. I wanted to help Mrs Clark, but when we heard him coming she made me hide. He was bullying her. Trying to make her give him money. I heard him, Tom, but please come now because I can't stand any more trouble."

She had hardly finished speaking before Mrs Clark jumped to her feet and, as Tom turned towards her, Jem leaned across the table and hit him. It was a badly-aimed blow, but it took Tom unawares, and he staggered back as much in surprise as in pain as Jem's fist struck the side of his head.

Jenny screamed, Macbeth barked and tore his lead out of Mary's hand, and Harriet rather obviously shouted, "Look out, Tom!" as Mrs Clark backed against the wall. But before Macbeth could go into action, Jem was on the floor nursing his jaw almost without knowing what had hit him. Tom with a slight smile, stood over him, rubbing the knuckles of his right hand.

"You're too slow, Jem," he said. "You're only good at bullying people weaker than you. Come outside and I'll give you another . . . OK, Mackie. Don't touch him. If you bite him, you'll be poisoned . . . Take the dog out, Mary. I'm just coming."

Tom was aware that Mrs Clark was begging him to go, begging him not to hit Jem – and suddenly he felt almost ashamed of himself. Then Jem said something about Jenny that made Tom look round quickly to see if the others had obeyed him. The girls had gone, but

Dickie was still standing in the doorway and Macbeth was again barking defiance from the pavement.

"Look out!" Dickie yelled as Jem scrambled to his feet, but Tom was ready this time.

"I'm looking forward to knocking you down again," he said quietly. Are you coming outside or are you going to have it here?"

Jem gave in. He sank down in the chair in which his mother had been sitting and put his head in his hands.

"You hit me when I wasn't looking. Get out and stay out."

Tom went without a backward glance. The front door was open and Dickie was performing a sort of war dance of triumph in the hall.

"Oh, boy! Oh, boy!" he chanted. "You hit him so hard and so quick he didn't even see it. Isn't he foul, Tom? Can't you see why we hate him?"

Tom put his hand on the younger boy's shoulder. "That's OK, Dickie. You can tell me the story on our way back."

He closed the front door behind him. The three girls and Mackie were standing by Jem's motorbike, and for a moment or two they were all rather shy. Then Tom laughed. "Nasty piece of work," he said. "Sure you're OK, Jenny? I want to hear how you got into that wardrobe. You can tell me on the way to the car park where I'm about due to meet Uncle Alf . . . Why, you're crying, Jen. Did he hurt you so much? Let me look."

He gently lifted the bruised wrist and suddenly she buried her face against his shoulder.

"My wrist doesn't hurt any more, Tom. I'm not really crying. It's just that I'm so pleased to see you. I've never wanted anybody so much in all my life as I wanted you when I was shut up in that horrible wardrobe. I thought I was going to die, Tom , and then I fell out and he went sort of mad and then I looked up and you were there..."

He put his hands on her shoulders and she raised her head and smiled at him as if there was nobody else there.

"I'm sorry, Tom. Have I been a fool?"

"Not any more than I have," he said grimly. "You don't know yet how I got here, do you?"

"If you two don't mind," Harriet interrupted, " I think we ought to go. He's watching us from the window, and although I know Tom would love to knock him down again I'm beginning to wish that we weren't here."

"I want to see his face when he tries to ride his bike," Mary said.

They had nearly reached the end of the street when they heard a motorbike starting up.

"Maybe he's coming after us," Dickie shouted. "Maybe he won't notice that he's got two flatties and he'll fall off. Oh, boy! What a day! Let's watch."

There wasn't much to see. As soon as Jem pushed up the wheel rest he must have noticed that his tyres were flat. They saw him stoop and examine them and then, to their delight, they saw him dance about in the road with rage when he saw them in the distance.

There wasn't time to tell Tom the whole story of "not scarlet but gold", but Jenny and Harriet between them gave him enough to keep him whistling with surprise.

"And you mean to tell me, Jen, that you took these three into the old mine last night without torches, when you knew that Jem and this other German bloke were in there? What's come over you lately? I'll have to talk to David about you, but, better still, I reckon I'd better come and look after you."

"I'd like that," Jenny said simply. "Why not ask Uncle Alf? I can see him over there by his Land-Rover. I hope he won't be cross because you've kept him waiting."

Alfred Ingles, who farmed close to Witchend, was very fond of the Lone Piners, and as Tom was an orphan he and his wife treated him like a son. Mr Ingles was a big, genial man who conducted most of his conversation at the top of his voice. When he saw the twins running towards him across the car park, his welcome was audible nearly a hundred yards away.

"BLESS MY SOUL!" he roared. "IT'S THOSE TWO COMEDIANS! HOW DID YOU GET HERE, MY DEARS? AND JENNY, TOO. Come and give your uncle a kiss, lass!"

Jenny was used to this. He wasn't her uncle and she hardly ever kissed anybody except her father, but she like Mr Ingles who smelled of his farm and shaving soap. He gave her a big hug which made her gasp and she gave him a shy kiss and then introduced Harriet.

Mr Ingles leaned back against his Land-Rover and looked Harriet up and down approvingly.

"Pleased to know you, Harriet. Jenny and Tom must bring you over to Ingles one day soon to meet my missus. If this lot says you're OK, then you're all right with us . . . What's that Tom, my lad? Can you what? Wish you wouldn't interrupt me when I'm talking to my girlfriends. Ha!! Ha!!"

Tom took his uncle aside so the others couldn't hear, but they noticed Mr Ingles suddenly look serious.

"Not quite sure what you lot are up to," he said when he came back. "Tom says he'd like to come back with you to Seven Gates and keep an eye on you all. You seem to have got mixed up in something serious. Tom can come now for a day or two, on the reckoning that you tell Charles Sterling what's been happening. Tell him too that I'll be over tomorrow or next day and have a word. Or he can telephone maybe."

Jenny smiled up at him.

"I don't know how much Tom has told you, Uncle Alf, but thank you for letting him come. We'll look after him. And I promise that we'll tell Mr Sterling everything – if David and Peter haven't told him already. Before you go, though, will you please tell us something important?"

Mr Ingles nodded. "If I can."

"Once, a long time ago, you told us what it was like up in these hills in the war. Didn't you say you were a sort of soldier as well as doing the farm? Didn't you have to guard the Mynd or something like that?"

"Yes, Jenny. And a rare lark it was too. Home Guards they called us and some odd bits of uniform we had and some excitement, too, I can tell you."

"Why did you have to guard the Mynd and the Stiperstones, Uncle Alf?"

He looked at her shrewdly. None of the others spoke, for they saw the sense of Jenny's question and waited, almost holding their breath for his answer.

"The Germans dropped spies and blokes to make trouble in the factories and to wreck bridges and railways," Mr Ingles replied. "Home Guards were out at night in lonely places like these hills to look out for them."

"Did you catch any, Uncle Alf?" Dickie said.

"We had some luck, but there were too few of us. We know for sure that many were dropped and some were never captured."

Jenny turned to the others. "You see, it's all true. This proves it. Let's get back and tell the others. Come over soon, Uncle Alf, and thank you for being so nice."

Mr Ingles climbed into the driving seat. "Take care of yourselves and no nonsense. I'll be over soon as I can."

They walked over to the bus station without saying much. Their bus had just arrived and Jenny smiled at a woman she knew as she got out.

"Hello, Jenny love. We've come through worst thunderstorm I remember. Hail, rain, lightning and what they call the lot. Road other side of Minsterley is under water, and you can't see top o' the mountain for cloud and lightning. Reckon that old devil is sitting on his throne right enough. Funny thing is you've had no rain here ... So long, all."

Jenny sat next to Tom in the back of the bus, and while they were waiting for it to start he said, "You've had quite a day, Jen, and it's not over yet. Sure you feel OK? Show me your wrist ... Wish I'd hit him again."

Jenny laughed. "I don't care, Tom. I don't care what's going to happen now. I'm glad I followed Mrs Clark. I'm glad you came and rescued me. I'm so happy."

CHAPTER 11

Peter and David

As soon as the others had gone off to Shrewsbury, Peter climbed on to the top bar of the gate again. "You can tell me what's on your mind now, David. I think I know, but you do the talking."

He looked up at her and smiled. "We really do want the large-scale maps, but apart from that, it's a good idea for them all to go off together. While they're in Shrewsbury, I'm going up Greystone to see if those two are still in the mine. I believe Jenny, of course, but I want to see for myself and make sure Jem and John have really gone. If they have, then we must hunt the hills whether they are exploring them or not. If they haven't gone after being discovered there last night, then I shall believe that they're already on the trail. See what I mean?"

"Oh yes, David. I see. We've hardly begun to explore all the old mine workings up there. It would take days to do it properly and we should want plenty of equipment . . . I'll tell you something that I wouldn't say in front of the others. There's something very horrid about it. Even if we found this German treasure I don't know what good that will do anybody. Even if we finally get the better of John and Jem, we're not righting a wrong, are we? There's Mrs Clark, of course, and I'm sure she's in trouble, but perhaps she'd rather be bullied by her son than have *us* interfering . . . This holiday started wrong for us, David, and I still feel it isn't going right. Harriet has got something when she says that we've not had much fun since we arrived. We haven't either. I do wish I didn't feel so unhappy about it all."

"You said you were happier about *us*. We're together again, aren't we?"

"Oh, yes. But I know you're going to suggest that you go into the mine alone. What am *I* supposed to do? Sit outside and knit?"

"That's not fair. You know as well as I do that John and Jem are dangerous. I want you to come up the dingle with me now, and then keep guard outside the entrance while I make sure that they're not where they were last night. If either of them come up the dingle while I'm inside, you can at least slip in and warn me. If we're both in there and they come back together, we might get caught before we could get out. There's only one way out of the mine now, so far as we know, and I don't want us to be caught *inside* by those two. They're ugly and dangerous, but you were keen enough at breakfast for us to go on with this business and we can't give up now. It wouldn't be like you to expect us to, would it?"

Peter jumped off the gate.

"I haven't been much like myself ever since we arrived, have I? I'm sorry you noticed. I'll come with you, David, but let's go as quickly as we can and get it over, and be sure we take the sort of equipment we shall need. Rope, food, macs, and all our torches and spare batteries. You get everything but the food together, and I'll cut some sandwiches and make some coffee," and she strolled over to the barn leaving David without words. Why was she so unpredictable? Peter had always been so straightforward, and now he still didn't know quite where he stood with her. Why couldn't she understand that he didn't want her in the cave because he was afraid she might get hurt? It might also be easier for one to escape, if pursued by Jem and John, than for two. He had an idea also that John would be ruthless if cornered.

After a few minutes David followed Peter into the barn and got his rucksack off the nail behind the big doors. She was whistling while she worked and didn't look up, so he said nothing. He found the torches, but there were no spare batteries. He packed in a coil of rope and then his anorak.

"Take your sweater, David," Peter called. "It will be cold inside the mine. I'm taking mine because it may be cold sitting outside with my knitting. I've enough food done to feed an army, I should think, so if you're ready we may as well go. No need to tell Charles or Trudie, I suppose. When the others come back with the maps, they'll guess where we've gone if we're not here."

David, with the laden rucksack on his back, led the way up the dingle. Thunder was rumbling round the hills again, and the atmosphere was thick and oppressive. David soon felt the weight of the rucksack and when they were halfway up he suggested a rest.

Peter sat beside him on a rock. He smiled at her, but she looked at him gravely until he felt awkward. After a little, he said, "The only way from the cave, with a motorbike, is down this path. If they came down last night or early this morning, they'd probably be carrying a lot of stuff and we ought to see their tracks. I've been looking out for the trail of tyres but haven't seen any. Have you?"

"No, I haven't, but the hills are running with water, and as it must have rained in the night any tyre marks would have been washed away. I've never seen so much water here nor the stream so full. And it's going to rain again soon."

It was true that the stream that ran down the side of the track was now a torrent and the water was often over the path itself. Both sides of the dingle were alive with little streams, while the shale and rocks glistened in the watery sunshine. David, although he wouldn't admit it, was tempted to turn back.

He got up from the rock, heaved the rucksack on to his back again and held out his hands to Peter.

A quarter of an hour later they clambered up to the little plateau outside the entrance to the mine and sank back exhausted against a rock. They had seen no sign of a motorbike's tyres.

David slipped off the rucksack.

"I'll leave one torch with you, Peter, just in case you have to come in and give me warning. I'm going straight to the pool where Jenny saw them last night. As I dare not show a light until I get there, or they give themselves away, it may be a quarter of an hour before I'm back. I hate leaving you alone here, but I promise that if they're not at the pool and I don't see or hear any sign of them, I'll come straight back here. If I'm in real trouble I'll shout a warning, and you'd better get back to Seven Gates as quickly as you can and tell Charles. I'm wondering whether I ought to leave the rucksack and the rope with you?"

Peter got to her feet and laughed.

"I can put your mind at rest on that one, David. I'd like you to take the rucksack, though it might be a good idea to wind the rope round your waist so that I can hang on to one end of it. I'll have one of the torches anyway because I'm coming in with you."

"But you promised to stay outside!"

"Of course I didn't, and anyway, if I did I only agreed to save a lot of argument. Please don't be silly, David. We've always done everything together and I'm coming in with you now. Truth is, of course, I'm scared to stay out here by myself, and even if anybody did come up the dingle, how could I warn you? I'm coming in and you'd better put your sweater on now. It will be cold in there!"

"I see. So that's why you brought yours too. And you needn't think I'd believe that you'd be afraid to stay out here, and I'm sure you'd find a way of warning me. All right, Pete. You win. Just one question I want to ask before we go in there. Please give me an honest answer. It's important."

"I promise."

"When we were back at Seven Gates, why did you agree so quickly to stay outside here?"

"Because I'm sick and tired of arguing and squabbling with you, David. I'm still not sure what has happened to us lately, but I'm not going back to the others today until we've sorted it out. I want us to settle this business of Jem and John first, because I've got a feeling that when we've done that we'll both be able to talk. I agreed to stay outside while you went in alone because it was the quickest way of getting you up here. I've made up my mind that we're going into this together as we've done lots of other things. That's the truth . . . You're very silly sometimes, but please don't talk any more now."

David smiled cheerfully as he wound the rope round his waist and handed her about three feet of its end.

"Drive the donkey into the cave," he said. "The water falling into the pool will probably be making a lot of noise, but don't talk or show a light. And keep close."

"Very well, sir," she said demurely, and followed him into the gloom of the old mine. As they did so, the thunder crashed and the light behind them was blotted out as a curtain of rain and hail swept up the dingle.

David went ahead carefully, with his left hand on the damp wall of the gallery, until his eyes became more used to the darkness. They went forward slowly, and gradually the sound of the storm outside was muted. After about sixty yards, Peter jerked the rope and whispered:

"We must be nearly at the turning now, David. Give me your hand. I hate the feel of this rope – it's unfriendly."

Soon they reached the entrance to the tunnel which ran quite steeply down to the pool. As they turned into it they were at once aware of a strong current of cold, damp air and the sound of falling water.

"Lots of water coming in," David said in a normal voice. "They won't be down here, Peter. Nobody could stick that noise and the spray for long. The pool must have been rising all night."

"It takes a lot of water to fill it, but we'd better go ahead and make sure. I agree that they'd be stupid to stay there, but if they are we shall see a light when we're round the next corner. Go ahead. Let's get this over."

There was no glimmer of light when they turned the bend, but the murmur of water was now a roar. When the passage widened, they walked side by side, and suddenly realised they were on the rocky ledge.

"They're not here," David said. "I'm switching on my torch."

"Wait!" she whispered with her lips against his ear. "Wait, David. I thought I heard a footstep behind us. Do you think they were hiding farther up the long gallery and have followed us down here?"

He pushed her against the rock at the back of the ledge, then edged along towards the entrance and went down on his knees and peered round the corner. He could hear nothing but the roar of the water and there was no warning light. He waited for a long minute, while some sharp stones dug into his knee. Then, with a grunt of pain, he eased himself backwards and bumped into Peter.

"All right, David? I'm sorry. I really thought I heard something. This place is getting on my nerves. Let's shine our torches down there. Now."

The two beams, like miniature searchlights, cut through the darkness on to the swirling water of the pool. Then they swung back and down to the little beach on which Jenny and the others had seen John and Jem last night. There was only about a foot of beach left now, but on the shingle were two empty corned-beef tins – and that was all. On this side of the water there was nowhere else to hide. On the other side, as they knew very well, was another cave at a higher level, through which the water was falling. And beyond that was another sloping gallery.

"I bet Jem would leave rubbish everywhere," Peter said. "Even in his bed, I expect, but I should think John is a tidy bloke and has taken his litter with him. Anyway, if they left anything else here it's at the bottom of the pool. What now?"

"Go back to the entrance, being very careful at the main turning – just in case you did hear something."

They went back, but David did not use his torch again until they were round the corner and into the main gallery, and soon they saw the faint glimmer of light at the entrance behind the big rock. It was still raining so they sat down on a patch of soft sand just inside.

"No sense in getting wet," David said, and Peter looked up at him in surprise because this was not the sort of remark he usually made and also because his voice sounded strained.

"I suppose not," she said almost as awkwardly. "Where do you think they've gone, David, and what shall we do now? I suppose they could easily be hiding in here somewhere. We know that, if we went straight on up this gallery and past the turning where some of the roof has fallen in, there are lots of passages we've never explored. The inside of Greystone is still a good place to hide in."

"I think we'd better call it a day," David said, without looking at her. "I've been thinking about this and I don't see much sense in searching the rest of the mine for them, and I'm not sure, Peter, whether we shouldn't give up the whole thing. I've an idea that young Harry is right and that we might be enjoying ourselves more if we kept out. See what I mean?"

She looked at him gravely.

"I don't think you mean what you say. Why have you suddenly changed your mind?"

"Don't make everything so difficult, Peter. I'm suddenly sure that I feel as you do about this place. I don't like it, and as I've nearly always told you the truth I'll admit that this looks like an ugly business and I don't want you mixed up in it. I didn't really want you to come for that reason. Both these blokes are greedy and I think they're both cruel. I admit I was jealous of John, but I'd rather call the whole thing off and just tell Charles all we know than have you concerned in anything so doubtful. Shall we go now?"

Peter shook her head, but her eyes were shining when he looked at her.

"It isn't very nice, I know, but we've got mixed up in it, just as we've found ourselves in an adventure before now, and I don't think we ought to run away from it. Thank you for thinking of me like that, David, but I like doing things with you – at least, I always have."

"What do you mean? Always have?"

"Just that. Now answer the question I'm going to ask you absolutely honestly. Suppose you were John Smith. You've got the clue. You're determined to find this money which, after all, your father wanted you to have. You're as sure as you can be that it's hidden somewhere round here – unless, of course, somebody else has found it by chance. You've tried to get somebody like me, who knows the hills, to take you round, and finally you've got Jem, who I suppose is the type who can be bribed to do anything, and is also being threatened because he fired Charles' hay. Then a lot of kids, as he's think of us, discover his hiding-place and escape before he can do anything about it. Now, David, what would you do if you were John? Honest answer, please."

David took her hand in his and looked down at her slim fingers. Outside the rain was still pouring down and they could hear the distant rumble of thunder.

"All right, Pete. You've caught me. If I was John whatever-his-real-name-is, I should be sure that Greystone Mine, right here, was a suitable hiding place. I should move my camp, as he has done, for it was a ridiculous situation anyway, and I should explore these galleries and workings for days if necessary. All the time I should be looking for signs which suggest 'not scarlet but gold' and trying to put myself in the place of my father, who I never really knew. This is exactly the sort of place which a man-on-the-run or one wanting a secret base would choose. I bet it's because the Germans knew about these mine workings that the spies were dropped here."

"So you wouldn't run away just because some kids found you? You'd find another, safer place to hide and explore every possible part of the mine with Jem."

"Yes, I would."

"Of course you would. So would I, and I'm sure we've got to search Greystone until we find them or can prove they're no longer here. Let's try and settle this business together, David. I've an idea that we shall be neither satisfied nor happy until we have. We can't give it up halfway through. When I was riding over here on Sally the other day and met John for the first time, I was sure this wasn't going to be the best of our holidays. I feel now that everything will be better for us when John and Jem are out of the way for good . . . And there's something I specially wanted to tell you, David, but you haven't seemed very interested to hear it . . . No! I'm not going to tell you now. Let's go in here and get it over. I want to beat those two to finding the treasure and then throw it at them."

David got up and pulled her to her feet.

"All right, Peter. I'm glad now that you're coming with me, but I wouldn't mind Tom coming along behind you to guard your back. There may be some stiff climbing over the rubble and stones in the gallery beyond the tunnel, but that's where we'd better try first. I think they'd get away from the water soon as they could after last night . . . We've no spare batteries, Peter, so save your torch. I won't use mine until we get past the junction and then you'd better hold on to the rope . . . I can't really remember what it was like up there except that it was dangerous."

"Let's try, anyway. If anybody else got by, I suppose *we* can."

The next fifteen minutes seemed like an hour. A few yards after they had passed the junction, the shaft, which had obviously been cut by hand, began to rise sharply. It narrowed, too, and there was only just room to walk in single file. The air was not as fresh as that in the tunnel leading to the pool, and David, picking his way carefully over broken rocks and stones, was soon perspiring and short of breath. He stopped, switched off the torch to save the battery and leaned against the rock wall, which was very wet.

"I'm puffed, Peter," he whispered. "Let's wait here for a minute and listen."

The darkness was as intense as the silence, which was

broken only by the thudding of his heart and Peter's quick breathing beside him. There was no other sound, not even the trickle of water which seemed to be oozing from the walls. It was impossible to imagine that there ever had been a sound in the heart of this old mine.

"This is the Devil's mountain all right," Peter said after a while. "I'm shivering now. Let's go on until we can't go any farther."

David switched on the torch again and they went on. The gallery swung to the right and now they could hear the trickle of water. A few more steps and they splashed through a shallow pool, and then David realised that they could go no farther. The passage was blocked by a fall of broken rock, and when he swung the beam of the torch upwards it disclosed a gaping hole where the roof had been. As they watched, a chunk of rock the size of a football shifted from somewhere up in the shadows. It moved with a crack and a scrunch and was suddenly falling towards them. It brought with it an avalanche of small stones and, although one struck him on the knee, the large rock which had caused the trouble bounded past them and splashed through the shallow pool in a thunder of noise, and down the slope up which they had just climbed. Peter, still holding the rope, dragged David backwards, but no more stones fell.

David wiped his forehead with the back of his hand and dropped his torch. It bounced off his foot and didn't break, and as he stooped to pick it up the beam showed him what looked like a scrap of paper at the edge of the pool, which was still rippling from the impact of the rock.

He picked it off the surface of the water.

"Hold the torch, Peter. Look! The paper isn't soaked right through. It's the wrapper off a packet of chewing gum and the printing is German."

PETER AND DAVID

"It couldn't be anyone but John," Peter whispered. "I remember he was chewing when I met him in the ruined cottage. I suppose he came as far as this and then turned back. He couldn't get over that fall or rock."

And then they had their second stroke of luck, for as David moved the beam back it lit up a gush of water coming from halfway up the wall between the pool and the pile of rock blocking the gallery.

"There's a hole in the wall there, Peter. Look! I believe it could be the entrance to another tunnel. Use your torch now and I'll try and climb up and see."

It was as David had suspected. He managed to pull himself up while the water poured down his legs. Then, suspended half in and half out of the hole, he used his torch again.

"It's OK as far as I can see, Peter. It doesn't look such a tidy gallery as the other – more like a narrow cave. We should have to crawl up because the roof is too low ... Look out. I'm coming down."

He slid back and looked ruefully at his jeans, which were wet through.

"I think there's a chance they went up there," he went on. "Will you stay here while I go up a little way and explore?"

"No, David. I told you that we're doing this together. Take off your rucksack and I'll pass it to you when you're up. If you can shove it behind you, you ought to be able to turn round and then haul me up."

Even without the rucksack on his back, it was difficult for David to turn round, but he managed it and then, by leaning over the edge and grasping Peter's wrists, he pulled her up through the falling water.

"We're crazy," Peter whispered with chattering teeth. "I'm beginning to think Harriet is right and that we'd be better out of this."

"Wish you'd thought of that before," David muttered as he began to crawl forward. "I'm mad too because we forgot to use the rope. I could have pulled you up with that and we wouldn't have got so wet. I'm going to use the torch now, Peter, but keep as close as you can and I'll let you know when I've had enough. Have you thought what we'll do if we come up against another rock fall? If we can't go forward and can't turn round, you'll have to crawl backwards... What a life!"

Peter said nothing. She was too wet and cold.

The shaft soon widened, but the roof remained too low for them to walk upright. The only sound was the constant trickle and tinkle of water, their own laboured breathing and the scuffle of their shoes amongst the loose rocks underfoot, but after turning a sharp corner David realised that the roof was high enough for him to stand upright.

"Rest, Peter," he gasped as he took her hand and pulled her up to him. She stumbled against him.

"Don't think I can do much more, David," she whispered. "I was a fool to think I could. This is a horrible place and if anybody finds any treasure in here they're welcome to it."

Before he could answer, they distinctly heard from somewhere above them the sound of tapping or of stone on stone. David switched off the torch and the thick darkness closed in on them like a clinging, velvet curtain. Then came other more sinister sounds from behind them as rocks began to fall from the roof. First a sharp crack, then a sudden gush of water followed by a crunch and the thud of falling stones. With horror David felt the wall at his back vibrating and then, with a fearful crash, the roof collapsed a few yards behind them. Instinctively he pulled Peter forward, pushed her to the ground and tried to cover her body with his own.

He did not even feel the pain as a piece of rock struck his ankle – all that he was conscious of was the horror of being such a fool as to have crawled up this gallery and to have allowed Peter to come too. Everything had gone wrong and, although he had never admitted it before, it seemed as if there was something in the idea that there was a curse on the Stiperstones. If ever they got out of this mess together, he'd be sure that they'd never come near the place again. He rolled clear of Peter into a puddle of water and realised that he was no longer holding his torch. There was an odd sort of scrambling noise above them and it seemed, although he could not at first believe his eyes when he opened them, that there was a flicker of light ahead.

"Peter! Pete!" he whispered hoarsely. "Are you all right? Say you're not hurt. Can you see a light?"

Peter sat up with her hand on his shoulder.

"I don't think I'm hurt. I suppose the roof's come down behind us . . . *Yes, David. There is a light. There's someone ahead of us.*"

David tried to get up but stumbled to his knees again as he felt the pain in his ankle.

"Lost my torch, Peter. Get yours ready. Don't switch on."

And so they waited, crouching fearfully on loose stones with water trickling over their legs, while the sound of stumbling footsteps came nearer and the glow of a torch, beyond a bend in the gallery, glistened on wet rock. Then there was another slither of loose stones ahead and they found themselves blinking in a dazzling beam of light shining into their faces.

"Mein Gott!" came a familiar voice behind the light. "It is the girl Peter . . . And the boy who came on the bicycle. You stupid fools! What have you done? Are there more of you? *Get out! Get out!*" and his voice rose

hysterically.

David felt his courage returning now that the suspense of waiting was over. He turned his head aside from the dazzling beam and got carefully to his feet.

"All right, John," he said. "Put out that torch for a minute and we'll tell you what's happened."

Darkness surged back and then David whispered, "Now, Peter. Get against the wall and show your light. Let's look at him."

Her light flashed on and for perhaps three seconds they saw John Smith standing about eight yards away at the corner of the gallery, with both hands at his sides but bending forward a little from the waist like a wrestler waiting to try a throw. He was wearing his leather shorts and they could see that his knees were scratched and grazed. But he was no longer the handsome, charming young man at whom a girl would look a second time. His hair was tousled and his face pale and streaked with blood. His mouth was open and his eyes gleamed horribly in the sudden glare. He picked up a rock and began to shout at them in German. Peter switched off as there came another rumble of falling rock behind them. When the abuse stopped, David said:

"We know you're German, John. We know a lot about you. Listen to me, if you don't want us all to be buried alive. If we shout or move too violently, we may bring down more of the roof. Have some sense, because I don't think we can get back to the main gallery. The roof fell in just now. Don't be a fool, John."

"OK," the German said. "Stay where you are. Are you two alone? Where are the other kids?"

"We're alone," Peter replied. "Where's Jem?"

"Never mind. Not here. How much do you know?"

"We know what you're looking for," David said

sharply. "What the three of us here have got to worry about now is how we're going to escape from here. What's behind you?"

John switched on his torch again, but instead of dazzling them he moved the beam up and down the walls and the roof.

"I won't move from here," he said quietly. "One of you turn round and see whether the way back is really blocked."

"Watch him, Peter, and don't move," David whispered, and then turned round and saw his own torch lying where he had dropped it. John, who had a very powerful lamp, kept his word and focused his beam on the pile of rocks which had so nearly crushed them a few minutes ago. Using also his own torch, which was now very dim, David looked with horror at the barrier between them and freedom. What seemed to have happened was that after a fall of smallish rocks, an enormous boulder loosened by water had crashed down, completely filling the narrow gallery.

He went back to Peter.

"Switch off and save your battery, John," he said quietly. "Stay where you are and we'll talk in the dark. We'll never be able to get back to the main gallery the way we came and there's so much water coming through the roof now that there could be another fall soon. What's behind you? What have you found? We're in this together now, John, and as three brains are better than two we may as well concentrate on getting out of here. What's above?"

John switched on the torch again and Peter turned her head away so that she should not be dazzled by the beam. David could feel her shivering. Then John began to speak. He was so excited that his almost too perfect English deserted him. It was obvious that he was still more interested in finding his father's treasure than in his own or anybody else's safety.

"I will tell you what is above, for only the three of us here know. It is important I have your help, for I have found a place where the money that is mine is hidden. I cannot reach it alone and that fool Jem is afraid and has gone off to the town to see his mother. I finish with him. He knows nothing and is all talk. Now you two will help me and I will give you a share of what I find and then I go back to Germany and that is the end of it all."

He paused for breath and then Peter answered him.

"You can have all the money, John. We've got to get out of here before more of the roof falls in. *What is behind you?*"

"I am nearly at the top of this passage where there is a big pile of broken rocks. With my light, through a crack between the stones, I can see what looks like a chamber. I am sure it is in there that my father hid the money for me. I cannot move all the rocks by myself, but you can help me." Suddenly he switched on the lamp again and moved the beam up and down the dripping walls. "There are red streaks on some of these stones and up here some look yellow. This is the place. I know it is. You must help me. Come now." He turned, and began to heave at stones they could not see.

"Stop!" David yelled. "Move the rocks carefully," but even while he was talking there was another fall behind them and the sound of a great gush of water.

"Crawl, Peter. Crawl as gently as you can behind me."

Slowly, painfully, they struggled up to the corner where John was now waiting for them. He helped Peter to stand up and then showed them both the barrier of broken rocks which he had begun to pull down. Then, through a hole between the stones through which he shone his lamp, they saw that on the other side was certainly a rocky chamber or another cave.

David nodded. "All right. Let's try and get through. You and I start on this, John, and move the rocks back as carefully as we can. Peter is going to find us something to eat from my rucksack. We've got some coffee too and that may help. Anyway, there's not room for more than two working side by side on this lot."

It took them two hours to get through the rock barrier. Peter moved back the stones shifted by David and John, who worked until their hands were bleeding and their eyes were stinging with perspiration. They were all strengthened by the coffee and sandwiches, but they wasted no breath in speaking to each other as they strained and grunted in the dimming of John's spotlight. When the last big rock was moved aside, it was typical that John should grab the light, push the other two aside and scramble first into what he hoped was some sort of treasure chamber.

Peter and David followed more carefully. It was a curious place – a sort of room about fifteen feet square. The floor was stone but the walls and "ceiling" seemed to be supported by pieces of rotting timber.

The place was empty. No treasure chest. No bundle of rotting banknotes. Nothing except stones and mud and the everlasting dripping water. The air was dank and stale. And there was no way out.

John turned on the other two in a rage. Again his command of English deserted him. He cursed in two languages, claiming that somebody must have got here before him and stolen what his father left for him.

David, so weary now that he could hardly stand, leaned back against the wall, put an arm round Peter's shoulders and told John to shut up. "Don't waste your breath, John. We've still got to get out of here and raving like this doesn't help . . . I think this place might be one of the old entrances to the mine and that we could be very near the surface. We've been climbing ever since we got inside. Stop behaving like a lunatic and let's all think what we're going to do."

Peter felt a sudden stab of fear at the expression on John's face as he stared at them. Then he put his spotlight on the floor and brought from the pocket of his leather shorts a big clasp knife and flicked the blade open.

"Very well then. We get out through the roof and start the search again," he said, and before they could stop him he climbed on a pile of loose stones against the opposite wall, reached up and began to hack with the knife at one of the balks of rotting timber.

"Stop that, you fool!" David shouted. "You'll have the roof down on us."

As John turned and snarled at them, the point of his knife must have struck a stone and turned the blade. With a cry of surprise and pain he dropped the knife and stumbled backwards. Then he shone the light on to his right wrist and watched with horror the blood welling out of an ugly cut. Then he dropped the light and crashed to the floor.

"Quick, Pete! Hold the light while I drag him over here. He's one of those blokes who can't stand the sight of blood."

It was a bad cut, but Peter knew enough about first aid to deal as sensibly as possible with John. They sat him upright against the wall and David pushed his head down to try to bring him out of his faint, but without much success. There was no bluster or charm about John as David cut strips from the sleeve of his shirt and Peter wadded them up and held them pressed against the wound until the bleeding stopped. David had a reasonably clean handkerchief with which they bandaged the wrist, and then with another strip they fixed John's right hand across his chest so that it was upright. Then David switched off the spotlight.

"We must save it, Peter. The battery is running out now and unless he has a spare we've only got yours. We can't do anything more for him now. Let's just rest for a bit. I'm sorry I've got you into this mess."

He put an arm round her and held her close. She gave a sigh which turned into a sob. Her head came down on his shoulder and he felt her hair against his cheek.

"I'm frightened. Are we going to get out of here? Nobody knows where we are . . . You see, if we're *not* going to get out I wish we could be alone together . . ."

He didn't answer at once. In the darkness he put up his free hand and touched her face.

"We *shall* get out. I think there's a way through the roof. There must be. This gallery wouldn't just stop here . . . You can't be more scared than I am, but I know we'll get out. Things aren't going to end like this for us, Peter. I'm sure they're not . . . What was it you specially wanted to tell me before we came in here for the second time?"

"Such a lot," she whispered, with her cheek still against his hand. "I shall feel braver if I tell you now. Do you remember our very first adventure at Seven Gates when I helped the gypsies?* Perhaps I never told you, but Miranda told me then that I'd have lots of adventures before I had my heart's desire. And now we're in this mess inside the Stiperstones that I've always hated, and I've suddenly realised that what she promised has come true . . ." She moved her head and he felt the touch of her lips on his hand.

"You don't have to be jealous of John any more, David. I don't mind you being jealous but I can't put up with you being so horrible to me by not writing, and

* Seven White Gates

being sulky about nothing . . . Can't you see that we're growing up and although perhaps I wasn't always sure what it meant, I know now that I've loved you from the day, up on the Mynd, when I first met you . . ."

Before David could answer there came from overhead an eerie groaning. He groped for John's spotlight and swung the beam upwards. The timbers across the roof were cracking. There came another indescribable noise as if the mountain was moving. *It was.* The roof was collapsing and the walls were bulging. He could feel the movement at his back and shouted, as Peter stifled a scream:

"Get back, Peter! Back into the tunnel." He thrust the spotlight into her hand, grabbed John under the arms and tried to get him on his feet.

"If you don't get back there, I'll leave him!" David shouted to Peter who was trying to help him. *"Do as you're told."*

And then there came a sickening, rending noise and a rush of mud and falling stones, and David was knocked off his feet as the light went out.

CHAPTER 12

Jenny Solves The Riddle

By the time that the Shrewsbury party were back in Barton Beach, Tom had been told the rest of the story of Jem and John Smith. It was fortunate that they had the top deck of the bus to themselves for most of the journey, because Jenny was constantly interrupted by the others.

Tom tried to be patient, but when he heard how Jenny had led Harriet and the twins into the old mine he beat his head with his fists.

"The whole lot of you seem to be crazy," he said. "Now you're sending me crackers too, because nobody can explain to me why? And what do you think you were doing, Jenny, going in that place as though those two toughs would welcome you with a pat on the head and a biscuit? It's about time I took charge of the operation. And what about Mr Sterling? Does he know anything about last night?"

"Not erzactly, we hope," Dickie explained.

Tom went on, "Soon as I've had a talk with David we'll have to tell Charles everything and I don't think he'll be very pleased with any of us. Seems to me that those two lads are really dangerous."

"Yes, Thomas dear," Mary said demurely. "We're sure you're right, but we wouldn't be surprised if David and Peter have gone to the mine just to see if Jem and John are still there. We know that Jem isn't, but where's John? That's the thing, isn't it? We've got the maps that David asked for, but we still think he wanted us out of the way . . . And another thing. We were very pleased to see you today."

A few miles south of Shrewsbury they ran into

153

another thunderstorm and noticed that low-lying parts of the road were under water. It was still raining in Barton and they sheltered for ten minutes in the post office, where Tom was greeted warmly by Mr Harman.

"Very nice to see you, Tom. Always welcome in Barton, my boy. Staying at Seven Gates with the others, I suppose? As you're here, perhaps you'd better go up and see Mrs Harman. Take him upstairs, Jenny love. Just to say 'How do'."

Tom was too polite to make any excuse. He was sure that Jenny's stepmother didn't like him, and she invariably pretended that she didn't know who he was. Truth was that, in an odd sort of way, Mrs Harman was jealous.

At last, between the storms, they hurried up through the wood to Seven Gates. The great doors of the barn were closed and when they opened up and trooped in there was no sign of David and Peter. There were a few embers at the bottom of the stove, and the twins promised to make up the fire and brew some tea while Tom went over to see Trudie.

He came back looking grave.

"Charles will be here soon. I'm going to tell him everything. If David and Peter went up Greystone soon after you left, they ought to be back by now. Why didn't they leave a note? Trudie doesn't know anything."

"They took food," Harriet said. "They left a bit of a loaf and the butter on the table. They made coffee too. Here's the jug with the grounds in it. Seems as if they expected to be away for some time, and it's about five o'clock now, I suppose. Don't worry, Tom. They can look after themselves."

Tom wasn't so sure. "Maybe they think they can. Anyway, I promised Uncle Alf that I'd tell Charles everything and I wish he'd come. We really have got mixed up in something this time and I think Charles is going to be angry."

"So do we," Jenny sighed. "Should we be doing anything now to help? Do you mean there ought to be a rescue party to go into the mine?"

"I think so," Tom said soberly. "I'm sure David and Peter know as much about this mountain as anybody and they've generally got plenty of sense. What I can't understand is why they didn't leave a message for you. That's not like David, because he's a tidy sort of bloke. I wonder if they took any equipment with them? Wasn't there a coil of rope kept behind the big doors over there?"

Dickie ran across to the open doors and pushed one back. "It's not there now," he shouted. "I saw it this morning. That shows for certain where they've gone. David knows it's dangerous in the mine, but he'll take care. They'll be back soon, Tom. Let's wait and see whether Charles comes home first. If he does, we'll tell him everything. If it's the others, Charles needn't know anything about it till David says so . . . Maybe we could have a celebration feast just to celebrate their safe return from foreign climes, if you know what I mean?"

Tom put down his mug of tea and walked over to join Dickie in the doorway.

"OK," he agreed. "We'll wait half an hour, but I reckon David would be back by now if he wasn't in trouble. I told Uncle Alf that you all seemed a bit out of your depth and were mixed up with some doubtful characters, and that's why he let me come today. One thing's certain sure and that is that we can't do anything on our own. We've got to have help."

It was Jenny's idea that while waiting they could easily make some more coffee and fill their flasks, because David and Peter would be sure to be glad of something hot. Then Harriet suggested that they might

NOT SCARLET BUT GOLD

look at the maps and see if any of the place-names suggested "not scarlet but gold".

"Of course, we'll look silly if they've found the treasure inside that awful mountain," she went on. "If they haven't found it, though, it would be good for us if we had one or two bright ideas about this silly old clue."

So they spread the maps on the table and, while Jenny and Tom got busy with the coffee, Harriet was fascinated by the Shropshire names of farms, hills, hamlets and villages of this lonely country. Romantic names they were, too. She read them out as she moved her finger across the numbered squares.

"Listen, Jenny," she said. "You know these places best. Tell us if they give you any ideas."

Jenny put the kettle on the stove and turned round.

"I've been thinking and thinking about this clue ever since it happened, Harry. You remember I asked my dad, too, but it didn't mean anything to him. I told Tom about it on the bus, and we're going to ask Uncle Alf Ingles when we see him again . . . All the time, though, I'm *trying* to remember something. Like waking up from a dream and fighting to get something back. And all the time that special thing gets farther and farther away. Do you know what I mean?"

"Yes," Mary said. "I know. I have dreams like that. Read out some names, Harry."

"I've found us," Harriet said triumphantly. "All the names I say now are round here. Giant's Cave, White Grit and Old Grit, which sound like mines but can't be anything to do with scarlet or gold. Then there's a place called Squilvers and another called Upper Grimmer—"

Suddenly Harriet rushed across to Jenny and dragged her over to the table.

"Look, Jenny. Could this be it? Cranberry Rock right on this very mountain. See. It's marked as clearly as the

JENNY SOLVES THE RIDDLE

Devil's Chair and Scattered Rocks. You showed us the last two but you didn't say anything about Cranberry. And Cranberries are red, aren't they? And red is scarlet near enough. Can you think of anything gold near Cranberry Rock? Is it the sort of place where a spy might hide something?"

"I suppose it is," Jenny agreed. "At least it might be if he was being chased and hadn't time to look anywhere else. I never thought of Cranberry Rock, but it's not nearly as high as the Chair. You can't get to it from Greystone without walking back from the top along the ridge. There is a big rock and thousands of broken stones too and they're very, very difficult to walk over. I suppose it would be possible to hide money under any of the rocks. Perhaps there's one special rock which is a golden colour. Are you listening, Tom? Maybe Harry has got a wonderful idea, but I suppose we can't go and explore Cranberry Rock this evening?"

"No, we can't Jen. And I'm not interested in all this business about a treasure. I want to be sure that David and Peter are safe . . . Suppose that gold has got something to do with sunset or sunrise? . . . This business gets madder and madder."

"Come to think of it," Jenny went on. "When I was in that ghastly wardrobe I heard Mrs Clark shout to Jem that she didn't believe there was a treasure and that John's father never hid anything, but perhaps she said that because she was sick of Jem bullying her. Anyway I agree with Tom—"

"*That's* a nice change," Mary said cheekily. "And now I don't think the treasure matters any more because I can hear a car coming up through the wood. If it's Charles, who's going to tell him about David and Peter?"

"Me, I suppose," Tom said. "My guess is that we shall be going up the dingle, in the Land-Rover, in about half an hour. I'm so sure, that we'd better make some more coffee and fill as many flasks as we can. And if Charles is mad with us, don't answer back. Specially you twins."

Dickie and Mary looked at him with disgust. Tom was getting as bossy as David and they knew from past experience that there wasn't anything they could do about it. They went to the doors of the barn and watched Tom open the gate in time for Charles Sterling to drive into the yard. They saw Charles wave his thanks and smile at Tom in surprise before driving into the shed which he used as a garage.

Tom admitted later that he had never known Charles so angry when he had been told that, although nobody *knew* where David and Peter had gone, they believed they were in the old mine. No sooner had Tom told him what they knew than Charles reversed the Land-Rover back into the yard and called the others over.

Then he made Jenny tell her story again. When she had finished by saying that they were sorry if they'd done the wrong thing, he went very white and said in a hard, quiet voice they had never heard before:

"Being sorry now doesn't help much. The lot of you seem to have lost your heads. You deceived me too because I should have been told this morning that some of you were in the mine last night. Can't you see that I'm really responsible for you all and now I feel I can't trust you. Seems to me that you may be using my barn for the last time . . . Jenny! Go in and tell Trudie how silly you've all been and warn her that I'm going to Greystone to look for those two foolhardy idiots. Tell her to get beds ready just in case they're in real trouble. Tom and you others can help me load up the Land-Rover. I want rope, spades and two pickaxes and levers, in case we have to move rocks."

Jenny, anxious to escape his wrath, dashed into the

house and then Charles turned on Harriet.

"Now, Harriet. You went into the mine first time yesterday. Is that right?"

She nodded, feeling very guilty.

"All right. Did you see any new falls of rock from the roof or walls of the galleries leading down to the pool?"

"It was dark and we hadn't a torch, but I don't think there were any fresh falls. Did you see any, twins?"

Dickie and Mary shook their heads.

"Good. What about the water? Was a lot coming over the fall and was the level of the pool rising?"

Harriet didn't know, but Mary said that the levels were not particularly high and then went on: "Please don't be so mad with us, Charles. We believe that Peter and David have been in the mine, but they might be on the way back now. And if they were in there they know all about the pool and how the water comes in."

"Maybe they do, but they don't know how much rock comes down in this sort of weather when the mountain is like a sponge. You two are as bad as the others and you'd better go indoors and stay there. See if you can help Trudie while we're away. Now, Tom. Let's check up and get going. We may need more than two, so Jenny and Harriet had better come if they promise to obey orders."

While Charles was striding about the yard stacking equipment into the back of the Land-Rover, they heard the blare of a car horn and an estate car drove into the yard. Jenny, who had just come out of the back door, was the first to recognise the driver.

"It's Uncle Alf!" she shouted. "Tom! Where are you?"

Tom came running from one of the barns with a spade and they all gathered round Mr Ingles as he got out.

"Hullo, all!" he roared and then shook hands with Charles. "How are you, Sterling? Thought I'd come over for a chat. Reckon you've heard that I met these youngsters in Shrewsbury and Tom told me a yarn about a young German and that waster Jem Clark. Something about bullying old Mrs Clark and making himself a nuisance and these kids going off into the mine last night. They all wanted Tom over here and it's good of you and your missus to have him. Anyway, the more I thought over this rigmarole, the more certain sure I was that I'd like to have a word with you. Did you tell Mr Sterling all you told me back there in town, Tom?"

"I've told him everything, Uncle. We believe that Peter and David may be trapped in the mine and we're going to find them. They left here with food after the others had gone this morning, but they didn't leave a message, so we don't know for sure that they're in there but we think they are. Will you come and help us, Uncle? We've got about everything we shall need in the Land-Rover and we can all travel up the dingle in that."

"COME? O' COURSE I'LL COME! Funny thing, but on my way back to Ingles, I got to thinking about this story and I didn't like it at all. That Jem never has been any good. He's a bad lot and now I hear he's set fire to your hay. Stupid little so-and-so. No time for him. Trouble always waiting just round the corner for him, I shouldn't wonder. TELL ME ABOUT THIS GERMAN. What's he doing and where is he now?"

"We'll tell you what we know on the way, and we'll be glad of your company, Ingles. Sometimes I wonder if this place is a nursery school. I'm thinking we'd all better go in the Land-Rover, for if the underground pool overflows like it did once before, there'll be a lot of water coming down the dingle and my Land-Rover will stand floods better than your car. We can't get very far up anyway."

"Reckon I'll follow you all the same," Mr Ingles said. "There's five of us and those two comical twins and

David and Peter and that's nine. I'll follow along."

"The twins aren't coming," Charles said. "What would they do if there's trouble in there? I'm afraid of roof falls after all this rain. If Peter and David went in without leaving a message, you can be sure they expected to be back here before this . . . Here's Trudie. She'll look after them. Darling, here's Mr Ingles driven over to see if he can help."

Alf Ingles shook Trudie's hand so hard that she winced. "I heard what you said about the twins, Charles," she said. "I believe you're not very pleased with any of them, but if you're all going up to the mine to search for Peter and David, you must take Dickie and Mary. They'll behave themselves, I'm sure, but they just couldn't believe their ears when you told them they were to stay here with me. You must know how devoted they are to David and Peter, and if those two are in danger the twins will break out of the house rather than not be with you. Please, Charles, I'll look after Mackie and I'll get hot drinks and such ready for you. Hurry up now, darling, and good luck."

They all watched Charles in silence. Then he smiled grimly and they knew he'd given in.

"I'll take 'em with *me,*" Mr Ingles said. "That's the best thing, and I'll keep an eye on 'em too. Send 'em out, Mrs Sterling, and trust me . . . No. Better still, I'll go and fetch 'em myself . . . Young rascals they be, but they've got *some* sense. I'll look after them."

So Mr Ingles went into the house for the twins, who were waiting just inside the door. They never told anybody what he said to them, but they were very subdued as they climbed into the estate car, just as the Land-Rover carrying the others and all the equipment drove out of the yard.

It was not possible to drive the car very far up the

dingle. The track soon narrowed and was strewn with rocks and the stream was now a torrent. When he could go no farther, Charles stopped and sent Tom back to speak to his uncle.

"Charles says it would be a good idea to turn here where it's wide enough. He could get up a bit farther in the Rover, but you'll get stuck in this muck. He says it might be a good idea to be facing the right way in case we have to get away in a hurry . . . So they've let you two out, have they? I hope you're going to behave yourselves," but at this last remark Mary gave him such a reproachful look that he looked really ashamed. When they jumped out, he put an arm round each of their shoulders.

"Sorry," he said. "Don't worry. We'll find them."

"Maybe we'll meet them coming down this old dingle any minute now," Dickie said hopefully. "If we do, we'll all look a bit silly, shan't we? It would be great if they'd come, though, because we could be angry with *them* for worrying *us* – just for a change."

They turned the cars and then the two men and Tom loaded themselves with the heavy equipment, leaving the girls to carry the haversacks and the torches.

"Mr Ingles and I are going on," Charles said. "You others are to do what Tom says, and if you don't get up to the entrance of the mine until we've gone in you're to wait outside. None of you, except Tom, is to go inside without permission. You've all of you been disobedient enough for one holiday, but I'm trusting you again. Look after 'em, Tom."

So the men went ahead and Jenny said, "Try not to look too bossy and important, Tom, because we just can't stand it. We want cheering up and not bossing about. Anyway, we're not going to be left far behind, even if the twins have to run," and Tom smiled although he wasn't feeling very cheerful.

JENNY SOLVES THE RIDDLE

The rain had stopped now, although thunder was still muttering away in the distance and the skies were clearing. Although they could not see the sun, its rays were lighting up the top of the dingle on their right. The atmosphere was heavy and depressing. Water was still trickling down the sides of the valley, and occasionally a few stones and rocks came slipping and bounding down the steep slope and splashed into the swollen stream which was swirling round their wellington boots and bringing with it plenty of mud and rubble.

"I know it's awful of me to say this," Harriet said suddenly. "I know you'll say I don't know much about your adventures, but WHY did we get mixed up in all this? I hate things to do with money like this, and anyway it's a stupid adventure and it's made us all unhappy . . . And now we've lost David and Peter and, come to think of it, *they've* been different ever since they came here."

"It's the mountain," Jenny said. "Tom always laughs at me, but that's because he wasn't born up here. Living over on the Long Mynd isn't the same. You'll never understand, Tom, but if you can't feel something hateful about this place right now, I'll never ask you over here again."

"Too late to be sorry about it all now," Tom said sensibly. "All we've got to do is find David and Peter, but I will say, Jen, that I don't like this place, although I don't believe a word about the spooks and the old Devil up in his chair . . . Come on, you twins. Can't you keep up?"

They waited for Dickie and Mary, both of whom were scarlet in the face and breathless. The former was furious.

"Of course we can keep up if our legs were as long as your legs are longer, you selfish beasts. *And* we put on our boots too, which are heavy."

Harriet laughed at them. "You're wonderful, Dickie.

You'll trip over your words one day. Words can be silly sometimes, like this stupid clue, 'not scarlet but gold'."

The two men were now well ahead just at the narrowest and steepest part of the dingle where the swollen stream was roaring right over the track.

Tom waved and shouted but they seemed not to hear, and were looking up towards the top of the scree where the setting sun was shining on a tree outlined against the sullen sky.

Jenny said, "I can't forget those words. I know they sound silly, but Peter was sure that they meant something important when she saw them written on the papers in the patchwork quilt. And John Smith thinks they're important too. We know that because we heard him say so last night. I think I *ought* to know what they mean. It's like waking up after a dream when you nearly had the answer to something which mattered. The trouble is that I can't quite — "

"Look! Look, Jenny!" Harriet screamed. "Look where the men are pointing. Something is happening up there."

Even while she was still speaking, the two farmers shouted a warning and began to run back towards them. Tom was the first to realise their danger. He grabbed the twins and pushed them back down the track.

"Run!" he shouted. "All run back. The dingle is moving. It's a landslide!"

None of them saw clearly what was happening during the next few horrifying minutes, for they were running for their lives. Later, when they could talk about it and all danger was over, they pieced together the complete story.

The part of Greystone Dingle which they had reached when the avalanche started was comparatively narrow with very steep sides. The two men had nearly reached a sharp turn to the right through a narrow gap between some rocks, which was only about one hundred yards

JENNY SOLVES THE RIDDLE

from the entrance to the mine. The Lone Piners, however, had only just got into this narrow section when Charles first noticed that a holly tree at the top of the scree was slowly sliding downhill. It was then that he shouted his warning and Harriet looked up to where he was pointing. The farmers, of course, need only have run forward a few yards to the safety of higher ground, but, realising the danger of being cut off from the others who were more vulnerable, they raced back towards them.

What happened was this. The side of the dingle, which was the steepest at this particular part, was shale – a mass of small rocks and stones with little soil to hold it together, and no vegetation except for the tree growing at the top. For weeks, thunderstorms had been rumbling round the hills and rain had been soaking into the soft sides of the dingle. The winter frosts had been severe and the thaw began the work of loosening the shale which, when soaked with water, began to slide over the layers of rock beneath it. All that this mass of muddy rubble could do was to pile up over the track and stream at the bottom of the dingle until its fall was checked by the opposite slope, but if any of them – particularly the twins – had been caught in its horrible clinging embrace, it would have been very difficult, and perhaps impossible, to rescue them.

At first the slip moved in an eerie silence. Beyond the warning shouts of the men and their slithering footsteps in the loose stones, the only sound was that of the swollen stream and the tinkle of running water down the scree. Then a few bigger rocks and stones came clattering down and splashed into the stream, and as the Lone Piners reached the safety of a rock jutting across the narrow path there came from all around them a horrible sucking noise. A huge lump – rather like cooling porridge – began to slide down with increasing speed and power, forcing before it an avalanche of loose rocks. Alfred Ingles, running fast and carrying a spade, was struck by one of these and bowled into the stream. Charles, a few paces ahead, heard his shout and helped him out of the rushing water. They reached the shelter of the rock just ahead of the mass of rubble, which slid sullenly across the track and smothered the stream in a cloud of spray.

Mr Ingles was more angry than hurt when Tom helped him to safety, but he was too breathless to say much. Charles, also puffing, threw down his spade and gave the twins, Jenny and Harriet, a quick smile.

"All OK? Well run, anyway. Get up on this rock and we can see what's happening. Safe enough here."

All that has been described since Charles shouted his first warning happened in about two minutes. As they clambered up the rock Jenny looked up again at the amazing sight of a holly tree, still upright, moving steadily down the hill, and then she suddenly solved the riddle that had baffled everyone since John's father muttered the words in his delirium in Mrs Clark's cottage many years ago.

As the golden rays of the setting sun caught the moving holly tree, she clutched Tom's arm and pulled him aside.

"I've remembered!" she shouted. "Now I know what the clue means. It's that holly tree. The one that's moving. Ever since I can remember we've cut berries from it at Christmas. *The berries are yellow, not red like the others:* not scarlet but gold! I can see a few on it now."

"Clever Jenny," Tom said, but not as if he really meant it, and then he turned to the two men. "Something very weird is happening up there, Uncle Alf. By the left of the tree. See? There's a whacking

JENNY SOLVES THE RIDDLE

great hole suddenly appeared in the ground."

Alf Ingles, still puffing and red in the face was rubbing his knee where the falling rock had hit him.

"What d'ye mean? Great hole? You're right, lad . . . Can you see it, Sterling?"

Suddenly Mary squeaked, "There's something horrible coming out of the hole. Dickie! Dickie! I hate it!"

Slowly, laboriously, struggling in the mud and stony rubble a slim, human figure dragged itself over the edge of the hole and stood for a moment looking towards them. Then, with a weak cry of, "Help! Come quickly. David's buried in the cave," Peter – for, of course, this bedraggled, courageous, exhausted figure was Peter – swayed and fell on her face.

"Come on, Ingles. And Tom. Bring the spades and the rope. We've got to get up there. You others stay here until we see whether it's safe to move across this muck. Do as I say . . . Listen, Mary. We'll get David, but we shan't be able to help him if you get stuck in the landslide. Look after them, Jenny."

Mary stared up at the horrible yawning pit in the ground in which her brother was buried, and beside which Peter had collapsed.

"Say prayers, twin," she gulped. "Help them be brave. God let Charles get there quickly . . . I can't watch them, Jenny! Tell me what happens," and she buried her face in Jenny's shoulder.

Dickie had no tears. He would have felt better if he had. His world was crumbling about him. In many ways he was more sensitive than his twin and he was now more frightened than he had ever been in his life. He looked away from Mary and at the two men and Tom struggling through the muddy rubble up towards the holly tree, and then felt Harriet's fingers close round his.

"Tell Mary what's happening," she whispered. "It's easier to watch. Be brave, Dickie. They'll be safe. I know they will. I just know they will."

So Jenny, with a quick look of gratitude at Harriet, held Mary close to her until her sobs quietened and they listened while Dickie, in a rather flat voice, described what he could see.

"I think the landslip has stopped moving now. It's all muddy, but Charles is in front and he's going quite fast ... Tom's just turned round and waved, but Uncle Alf has fallen down again. I think his knee hurts him ... Now Charles has nearly reached Peter, but the last bit is very steep and slippery ... Look, Mary! *Peter is getting up* ... She's OK, I think. Charles is shouting something. Now he's there and they've gone crackers and are hugging each other ... You can stop snivelling now, twin, and see for yourself ... *Hi! Peter!! We're all here. Up the Lone Piners!*"

Mary did as she was told and turned to see what was happening. The rescue party was gathered round Peter, who was pointing behind her into the pit. Charles and then Alf Ingles lowered themselves carefully into the dark hole.

"Come across now," Tom shouted. "Peter's OK and we'll soon get David up. Can you hear me, Jenny?"

"Yes, Tom. What shall we do?"

"If you move carefully, one behind the other, you shouldn't slip. You first, then the twins, and Harry last. Don't panic, but if you feel you can't go on, stay still until I fetch you, but we want the rope for David. Bring the haversack, Jenny. We'll want the coffee soon ... OK?"

"OK, Tom. We're coming," Jenny shouted. "Can you hear us, Peter? We're on our way," and then to the others, "Don't worry, twins. David will be all right. I'll take this haversack and Harry the other and you follow where I go. Isn't Tom wonderful?"

Jenny said the last words so seriously that even Mary laughed, and then they all cheered excitedly when Peter waved to them before going back to the edge of the pit.

The climb up was nerve-racking but not particularly difficult. Jenny, now taking the lead, picked her way carefully as she had seen the men do. It was muddy and slippery, but the others followed her fearlessly.

"Don't look down or behind you," she warned them and then shouted to Tom, "We're doing fine. Don't wait for us. Go and help the others."

The momentous few minutes which it took them to reach Peter provided a wonderful fund of material for Dickie when he told the story of their exploits later. Sir Edmund Hillary, the conqueror of Everest, might well have blanched at the risks taken by the brave Morton twins!

But the truth was that neither of them lost their heads, and because they were now actually doing something to help they behaved splendidly. Harriet, too, was a tremendous help and might have had many adventures like this before. Tom, with a slightly anxious look at Jenny's tense, freckled face, called out, "Take it easy then," and scrambled up a few yards to where Peter, on her knees, was looking down into the pit.

Another minute and they were safely there, and as they struggled up the last few feet Tom called over his shoulder, "David's OK. He's coming up now," but Peter didn't even turn round to greet them.

They found themselves looking down about twelve feet into a square chamber cut out of the hillside, the "ceiling" of which had collapsed in a welter of mud and rotting timbers. In the far corner was the entrance to a tunnel where, to their astonishment, Charles and Alfred Ingles were supporting the muddy, blood-streaked figure of John Smith. But far more important was that David was already climbing up towards them, and as he grasped Tom's hand he gave them a grin.

They hauled him up and he rolled over the edge and then sat up and spat out a mouthful of mud. Peter was on her knees beside him.

"I don't know how I got out, David. Suddenly I could see the sky and when I managed to get up here, there were the others over there with Charles and Mr Ingles. It was like a miracle. Are you all right, David? Do you realise we're safe?"

Jenny noticed the look David gave Peter as he took her hand and held it against his cheek. Then, when he saw the tears on Mary's face, he dropped Peter's hand and put both arms round his sister and gave her a kiss.

"Come on now, Mary," he said. "Unpack that food and give Peter a hot drink. John will want some because he's not quite himself and I could do with a little something too . . . I suppose I'm dreaming, Jenny, but it looks as if you've collected Tom from somewhere. He looks real to me, he seemed real when he hauled me up and he spoke as if he were Tom."

"It *is* Tom, David. Really it is. He rescued me today in Shrewsbury and now he's rescued you."

"Good old Thomas! Hullo, Tom. Nice to see you."

"Silly fool," Tom grinned. "You two have given us plenty of trouble I must say. I suppose this other character is Jem's nasty friend. It'll be interesting to know how you got down that hole with him."

"We didn't get down. We came *up,*" Peter tried to explain. "Oh, thank you, Harry. I don't think I could eat anything, but coffee will be wonderful."

While she was talking, the two men had got John over the rubble and were now standing directly below them. John's wrist was still strapped to his chest, but his

JENNY SOLVES THE RIDDLE

arm was bloodstained and his face white under a layer of mud. He seemed only half-conscious and his head rolled as he tried to speak.

"Throw the rope down, Tom," Charles called. "We'll have to haul him up, I think. David and Peter OK?"

They got John up without much difficulty and propped him against a rock while Peter gave him hot coffee. He tried to smile again and muttered something in German which sounded like "*Danke schön.*"

"We must get him to a doctor at once," Charles said. "That cut will have to be cleaned and stitched up . . . Will you take him in your car, Alf? Take the twins, too, and drop them at Seven Gates and they can warn Trudie about baths and beds for Peter and David. I'll follow with the others as soon as you're away."

Mr Ingles nodded. "Hospital in Bishop's Castle is the nearest, I reckon. How to get him across this muck?"

"He'll have to walk between us on the rope," Charles said grimly. "Do you understand what I'm saying, Whatever-your-name-is? We're taking you to a doctor or a hospital and you've got to walk over to that rock. You've got to make the effort. Understand?"

John nodded and struggled to his feet.

"Now," he said. "We go now," and then to Peter and David, "You saved my life. How do I say thank you? I see you again, yes?"

"OK then," Charles said. "Let's go . . . Can you manage by yourselves, twins? Don't hurry till you're safely over and then run to Mr Ingles' car. Tell Trudie what's happened and that we'll be along with two more casualties in a few minutes."

Dickie, very serious, nodded and took his twin's hand.

"Don't you worry, Charles. We'll be at Seven Gates first. Trust us, Charles . . . See you all soon," and they crossed confidently down to the safety of the rock and then disappeared to the path below.

"You others come as soon as we're over," Charles said. "I'll wait if you're in trouble, but I want you to hurry because I'm wondering when the stream under all that mess is going to break out . . . Now, John. If you feel you're going to slip or can't make it, just shout, but the rock surface is too slippery to risk carrying you. The rope will hold you, but keep your wrist upright if you fall."

John nodded, squared his shoulders and followed Mr Ingles. He stumbled twice and slipped on his back once, but Charles hauled him up and held his undamaged arm for the last ten yards.

"We can manage, Charles," David called as soon as they were over. "Wait for us at the Land-Rover."

Harriet began to pack up the haversack, but Peter, who was now very pale, said *"Please* don't fuss about that now, Harry. We can come back tomorrow. I shall flop down here if we don't get home soon."

Five minutes later, weary, footsore, bedraggled and half asleep they reached the Land-Rover.

"Peter and David in front with me," Charles said, as he swung first Harriet and then Jenny into the back. "Hold on to Tom, girls. You're going to have a bumpy journey."

It was dark now and the headlights of the Land-Rover threw strange shadows against the rocks and the trees as they lurched down the rough track. When they drove into the farmyard, Peter was asleep with her head on David's shoulder. The twins, followed by Mrs Sterling, ran out to meet them.

"Let me see to Peter first," Trudie said. "Charles, I'm sure none of them should sleep in the barn tonight. We daren't trust them out of our sight. The twins can

JENNY SOLVES THE RIDDLE

sleep in the sitting-room in their sleeping-bags, Tom and David in the big guest-room and Peter in the other. Jenny darling, could you take Harriet home with you for the night if Charles drives you down to Barton? Mrs Harman won't mind, will she?"

Jenny wasn't so sure, but no doubt Charles could persuade her stepmother if anybody could.

"Do you mind, Harry? Oh, good! I'd love to have you," she said as she jumped down.

David and Peter came over and the latter said, "I'm hardly awake now, but come up early as you can in the morning, Jenny and Harry . . . So much to tell you . . . And thank you for being so wonderful today . . . Good night."

Jenny suddenly realised Tom was standing next to her.

"Tom. You've forgotten that I'm sure I've solved the riddle and I don't think the others heard me. If there's a treasure, it will be under that holly tree – the tree with the yellow berries still on it. I saw them when it was moving. I wanted to stay and search when we were up there, but, of course, I couldn't . . . I'm going to take Harry up there before breakfast. Will you come along too so that we can find the treasure together? We'll meet you in the dingle at eight o'clock."

"You won't be awake, little redhead," Tom teased, and ruffled her hair. "We've had quite a day, Jenny . . . Don't be late in the morning."

CHAPTER 13

The Treasure At Last

Next morning Harriet was rudely awakened by the shrill clamour of an alarm clock. When she opened her eyes she saw Jenny leaning over her. Then she remembered. She was in Jenny's house, in Jenny's bed and wearing a pair of Jenny's pyjamas. She didn't remember very much about happened after Charles Sterling brought them last evening, because she could hardly keep awake, but had a dim memory of Mr and Mrs Harman, scrambled eggs and cocoa, and a hot bath. She opened her eyes still farther and pushed Jenny back on the pillow.

"Hello, Jenny," she yawned. "Why did you make that horrible noise? I could go on sleeping for a day and a night."

"I'll tell you why. I've got a surprise for you. We're going up Greystone again and meeting Tom at eight."

"Oh, no!" Harriet wailed, snuggling down into the bedclothes again. "Please NO, Jenny. I know Tom is wonderful, but I don't want to meet him before breakfast . . . Anyway, you don't want me if you're going to elope with him."

"I wish I was," Jenny said fervently. "You're being silly, Harry. It's the treasure. I know where it is. I know what 'not scarlet but gold' means. It's a holly tree with yellow berries. It's the holly tree that slipped down the dingle and I'm sure the German treasure was hidden somewhere close. It might be in that ghastly hole, of course, but I hope it isn't. Anyway, I told Tom when I thought of it and he said I was clever. Then I remembered it again last night at Seven Gates and asked Tom to meet me there this morning and he said

THE TREASURE AT LAST

he would. And I want you to come because you thought I didn't like you and didn't want you in the club. But I do. Both those things. So that's why I set Dad's alarm because I thought you'd like to share the finding of the treasure and we must go early before the others get up. I want to surprise them. Are you excited? Will you come?"

"I am and I will, Jenny. Thank you for asking me. Will your parents mind if we go before breakfast?"

"By the time we're downstairs, Dad will be doing the papers and having a cup of tea. We'll have one with him if there's time. Hurry up," and Jenny jumped out of bed.

Harriet groaned and followed her.

"I'll come in the bathroom with you, if you don't mind," Jenny said. "We shall have to hurry and you might be frightened of the tap."

"Why should I be scared of a tap? I wasn't frightened last night."

"It's difficult to explain, but the hot tap is most peculiar. Sometimes when you turn it on it goes *bom-bom-bom-bom* ... Come on, let's go and try it."

It went *bom-bom-bom* and the house shook. Harriet was fascinated. Mr Harman wasn't particularly surprised to see them ten minutes later. They had a cup of tea with him and then Jenny gave him a kiss. "Tell Mum I've made our bed and we'll see her soon, but we had an early appointment for breakfast at Seven Gates. 'Bye, Dad."

It was a beautiful morning. Fresh, clean and sunny, and when they looked up at the mountain they could clearly see the Devil's Chair.

"It's a quarter to eight and we must run," Jenny gasped. "We mustn't keep Tom waiting. Won't it be wonderful if we find the treasure?"

Soon after they turned into the lane that led into Greystone Dingle. Harriet had not been this way before, and because she had a stitch she stopped to look over the parapet of a little bridge.

"Is this the stream that comes all the way down from the top, Jenny?" she asked. "The one we splashed through last night? It's disappeared."

"It's got stopped by the landslide, of course. Didn't Charles say last night that we must hurry because it might suddenly burst through and come with a rush? We must warn Tom."

He was waiting for them by the old signpost where three tracks met.

"I could hear you two chattering about half a mile away," he smiled. "You're late, so let's get going. I'm hungry."

"Oh, dear," Jenny sighed. "I do wish you could be more romantic, Tom. Here we are meeting early on this lovely morning and we're going to find a treasure that's been hidden for nearly twenty years by a spy who's dead now but was probably a very nice, kind spy – and all you can say is that you're hungry. Acksherley, as Mary says, I thought you were rather nice to me yesterday."

"Would you like me to walk by myself?" Harriet suggested without a smile. "Tell him about the stream if he hasn't noticed. And I'd like to know how Peter and David are?"

"David doesn't even know I've gone out," Tom replied. "He was asleep as soon as he got into bed. He looked quite like David after he'd had a bath. He said he was bruised all over though. I didn't see Peter. Trudie whisked her off after saying that we all ought to be ashamed of ourselves, which I thought was fair enough. I've left a note to say that I've gone out to meet you two ... What's this about the stream?"

Jenny explained.

"Yes, of course," Tom agreed. "Perhaps that narrow

part of the dingle is dammed and filling with water? Perhaps your holly tree is floating by now, Jen? Perhaps your treasure is sunk. We'd better go and see. And if we hear the water coming down I'll race you both up the side of the dingle. So look out and let's go."

Almost before he had finished speaking they heard a dog bark, and when they turned round there was a black Scottie dashing down the track from Seven Gates.

"It's Mackie!" Jenny cried. "I bet the twins are just behind. Hullo, Mackie! You are a clever dog to find us. And here are the twins."

Dickie and Mary were running, but as soon as they saw the others they slowed down to a dignified walk. They were very hot and breathless when they came up and seemed to be only half-dressed.

"Come here, Mackie," Mary said. "Don't speak to them. They're unworthy."

"Good morning to you all," Dickie added coldly. "Fancy meeting you here. S'traordinary thing. So early in the morning. And would you by any chance be strolling up the dingle this morning because if so, we would prefer to go ahead and not accompany you."

"So what?" Tom grinned. "So what do you intend to do in the dingle and why have you come?"

"You, Thomas," Dickie said, "are a skunk."

"That's right," Mary added. "A skunk that slunk away without telling his friends. A smelly, selfish old skunk. If you were going to meet Harry and Jenny, why didn't you tell us?"

Jenny giggled, but Tom said, "You two are much too cheeky and I've had enough of it. How did you get here, and what do you mean by following me around?"

Dickie said patiently, "We followed you because we want to know why you wanted to meet these girls. *And* we knew you were going to meet them because we read the note you left on the kitchen table for Trudie, *and* we knew you were up to something because you made such a row getting up that you woke us up."

"*And* that's the truth," Mary added. "Have you got a secret to share with us, Jenny? We think you have, and we shall follow you to the end so you may as well tell us now. We've left a note for Trudie, too, just to say that we shall be a bit late for breakfast."

Tom laughed. "I can't fight you two."

So they set off up Greystone together and Jenny told the twins how she had suddenly remembered the holly tree with golden berries, which she believed was where John's father had hidden the treasure. The twins were very impressed and forgave Jenny for not telling everybody all about it last night. They were also quite gracious to Harriet realising that as she had been sleeping in Jenny's room it would have been difficult to leave her behind this morning.

They reached the place where the cars had been left last evening. Tom noticed that a lot more water was coming down the stream. It was very muddy, too.

"We must climb up higher," he warned. "I think it's going to break and if it does it will be quite a sight. Keep Mackie to heel, Mary. He could get washed away in the flood water."

"Our dog is very obedient, thank you, Tom As you should know very well after he rescued you and Jenny yesterday. And we would like to see the water come down with a rush if it doesn't hurt anybody anywhere."

Mary had her wish. They were halfway up the slope when the mass of mud and stones piled up by the pressure of rising water burst with a sullen *thrrrrump*.

In a few seconds the rock to which they had run for safety last evening was hidden in spray as the released water forced rocks and shale and mud into the bed of

THE TREASURE AT LAST

the stream, where it rushed like a tidal wave, tearing at the banks and uprooting bushes on its way.

The twins cheered, and Harriet said, "We'd better hurry, Jenny, because your golden tree might start sliding down again." At this fearful warning, Jenny grabbed Tom's hand and and dragged him up towards the ridge of rock beyond which the landslide had started. They were first over in spite of the twins' protesting cries, but Jenny would not even wait to look at the amazing scene at the foot of the dingle where the power of the hidden water was moving the rubble of the landslide like bubbles in a witch's cauldron.

The holly tree was still upright, although some of its roots were now exposed.

"You really are a clever girl, Jenny," Tom said when he saw the golden berries. "I can guess that a bloke on the run with something valuable to hide would choose a landmark which was easy to remember. But where would he hide it? Under the roots if he was in a hurry? But maybe he'd found the secret chamber and hid it there? This is your affair, Jenny. You look first and I hope you find it. Good luck."

She flashed him a smile and then, as the others clambered over the rocks behind them she scrambled across to the tree.

"I only want Mackie," she called. "Lend him to me, Mary. I want him to dig."

The holly tree had slid down the side of the dingle because the soil in which it was rooted had slipped in one lump. Jenny went down on her knees and grubbed about under the roots, and then Mackie, urged on by the encouraging cries of the twins, began to dig furiously. When his mouth was so full of dirt that he could hardly breathe, Macbeth emerged. He coughed, shook his head, and then plunged again into the hole already made, and with yelps and whinings returned to the hunt of he knew not what. It was fitting, perhaps, that Macbeth should find the treasure and that Jenny should drag it out from between the roots of the holly where it had been hidden for so many years.

The others crowded round as she held up a parcel wrapped in what might once have been yellow oilskin.

"What *is* it, Jenny?" Mary squeaked. "Open it. Is it jewels rich and rare without compare, or little leather bags of gold? *Open it!*"

Jenny tore off the rotting layers of oilskin and then held up two bundles of ancient, one-pound notes. The notes were damp and soiled at the edges.

"Millions of pounds!" Dickie gasped. "Is it real?"

"Real enough, I bet," said Tom, who, like Dickie, had never seen so much money before. "I wonder who it really belongs too? To John, I reckon, and we don't know how he's feeling or where he is this morning. Anyway, you've hit the jackpot, Jenny, and if you hadn't remembered the tree when you saw it yesterday nobody else would have found it. John never would. I don't think you'll be allowed to keep the money."

"*I* don't want any of it," Harriet said quickly. "Bringing it over here has killed a man. Then it brought the hateful Jem and John together. Jem bullied his mother and did horrible, cruel things and John came over here specially to find it, and whatever else he was he told lies and made Peter unhappy and we know he bullied Mrs Clark too . . . I'm sorry to say all this, Jenny, when you're so excited and you've been so clever. Let's go back and tell the others and see what they say. I bet David and Peter will think you're wonderful too."

Jenny looked rather crestfallen but they all knew that Harriet was right.

"We shall have to tell Charles and Uncle Alf," Tom

THE TREASURE AT LAST

said. "We'd all better stuff some in our pockets. We may as well walk about like millionaires once in our lives." So they went back down the dingle, carrying the money which was to have been used to bribe traitors when Britain was in peril. They had to keep well above the track, which was now covered with a mess of rubble, uprooted bushes and muddy water, but they were able to hurry when they reached the signpost and turned left up towards Black Dingle and the farm.

Mary ran ahead and so was the first to give their news to Seven Gates. For once Dickie didn't seem to mind his twin's desertion and wasn't surprised to see her waiting with Charles when they hurried into the farmyard.

"Oh goodness," he said to Jenny. "Here's Charles. I do hope he's not mad with us again, but Mary is laughing, so perhaps she's made it all right . . . Good morning, Charles! Have you heard we're millionaires? Jenny solved the riddle and we've got the lolly. And if you'll excuse us saying so we hope we're not too late for breakfast."

Charles nodded amiably.

"I should think we've suffered enough from you all in this house since you arrived, but Trudie is hoping you'll stay to breakfast. How much longer we can put up with you all, I'm not sure. David is probably down by now, but Peter is still sleeping. Come in and let me see what Richard so inelegantly calls the lolly. You can talk as you eat, and I want the true, full story from you before we send you all packing."

"Dear Charles," Mary smiled. "You've forgiven us! You are my favourite man and we know that you're not really going to send us out into the cold, hard world. P'raps you can have another breakfast with us?"

They surged into the kitchen and emptied their

pockets of the lolly on the end of the table.

"Millions and millions of pounds!" Dickie chanted. "Just look, Trudie. Clever Jenny found it in a parcel under the holly tree."

Trudie was unimpressed.

"So I hear. But I shan't forgive you until you've eaten your breakfast and I know that Peter is all right. You've been a worry to everybody, when we're supposed to be responsible for you . . . Will you please clear all those nasty notes off the table, Charles? And Alfred Ingles telephoned while you were outside. He's coming over presently after he's been to the hospital where he left that German boy last night. He wants to talk things over, and I'm not surprised."

Charles nodded, helped himself to a cup of tea and began to count the money. The others settled themselves at the table and then David arrived. He was limping and had a big bruise on his forehead. He went over to Trudie, who was still at the stove scrambling eggs, and apologised for being so late. Then he looked round the table and saw Charles counting ancient notes and the others watching him expectantly.

"I found the treasure this morning, David," Jenny said quietly. "I suddenly realised that 'not scarlet but gold' was a holly tree with yellow berries and it was close by that horrible place we rescued you from. We went up there this morning and I found – Tom helped me – all that money."

"Good for you, Jenny," David said, without a second glance at the notes which Charles was counting. "And before breakfast too! Where's Peter? Have you seen her this morning, Trudie? Is she all right?"

"I think so, David. She was still asleep when I went up half an hour ago. I want her to sleep on, but I'll take her some breakfast when you've been fed. I'm not very

THE TREASURE AT LAST

proud of you all for getting yourselves into this ridiculous adventure which didn't really concern you. How do you feel yourself?"

"Sore," David said. "I'm sorry we've been such a nuisance, Trudie, and thank you for being so decent about it all. It got out of hand, but I know I'm to blame for taking Peter off yesterday and not leaving a message."

Trudie gave him her sudden smile, passed him a plate of bacon and scrambled eggs and then led him over to the window.

"I wouldn't be surprised if *she* took *you*, David! Have your breakfast and don't worry. I'll tell her presently that you were asking after her and, although it's no business of mine, I should think it's about time you two had a straight talk. She hasn't been very happy this holiday, has she? Has she told you that her father is leaving Hatchholt and going to live with Charles' father near Hereford?"

David nearly dropped his plate.

"No! *Why* hasn't she told me? She *can't* leave Hatchholt. It's her home."

"She must. You two are growing up, David, and *you* don't seem to realise it. You'd better not let her know I've told you this. Give her the chance to tell you herself . . . Now sit down and eat your breakfast and don't look so miserable."

David did as he was told and, although the others had not overheard his conversation with Trudie, they all realised that he wasn't listening to what they were saying.

"Several thousand pounds in Bank of England Treasury Notes here," Charles said. "We've got to decide what we're going to do with it. Meanwhile, David, we want to know exactly how you got into this mess yesterday while the others were misbehaving themselves in Shrewsbury."

The others sat spellbound while David described the horrors of the dark tunnels, the water and the collapse of the roof. He praised Peter's coolness and courage, of course, and when he tried to describe their crawl, in running water, up the shaft to where John was waiting for them, Harriet covered her face with her hands. He told them, too, of how John behaved in the last few minutes before the roof of the chamber fell in – of how he cut his wrist and how he fainted and of how Peter stopped the bleeding. But he told them nothing else.

"I see," Charles said quietly. "Thank you, David. You're all a lot of foolhardy young idiots, but you all acted with resource and courage. Any of you will always be welcome at Seven Gates, but you will promise me NEVER to go into Greystone Mine again. You promise? . . . Very well then. I've got to decide what to do about this money. It might be counterfeit – might have been printed in Germany. When we know what's going to happen to John Smith, we'll have to decide about Jem Clark and his mother. Meanwhile, you go and tidy up my barn. Be off with you," and, rather chastened, they all went out into the sunshine.

"What do you think is going to happen to John?" Jenny asked David. "Was he really badly hurt?"

"I don't think so. He's scared at the sight of blood and anyway he was half crazy over the idea of the money. It doesn't matter if we don't see him again, does it? Or Jem. I'm sorry I got you all in such a mess yesterday . . . We can't decide what to do until Peter comes down, can we?"

"Uncle Alf is coming presently," Tom reminded them. "He'll have news of John, too. Why don't you go up and see how Peter is, Jenny? Tell her we can't do

THE TREASURE AT LAST

anything with David until she comes down." Jenny winked at him and ran in, and soon after Mr Ingles arrived with John.

They all went into the farmyard when they heard the car coming up through the wood. Mr Ingles waved a greeting before getting out, but John stayed in his seat. He was very pale and his arm was in a sling.

"Hullo all," Mr Ingles roared. "Pleased to see you up and about, David. Not much the worse, I hope. Peter OK? Where's my Jenny girl? Hullo twins . . . And Harriet! This bloke John will be OK. They've cleaned him up and given him a good night's rest and now he's discharged. Said he wanted to come up and see you all. Odd sort of fellow. Can't make him out."

As usual, Mr Ingles made all these remarks at the top of his voice, but although John could not help hearing the last comments he made no sign but sat staring straight ahead.

Then Jenny came out with Charles and Trudie. Charles was carrying a bundle of Treasury Notes.

He stopped when he saw John, called Jenny back and tossed her the money.

"You found it, Jenny. Hold on to it until we decide what to do. Hullo, Ingles. These kids found all this cash this morning under the roots of a holly tree up by the landslide. Jenny solved the clue. Come into the barn and we'll tell you about it and then we'll want to know why this German chap has come back . . . You, John – whatever-your-real-name-is – come in here. We shall want a lost of answers from you."

Meanwhile, Trudie had gone over to David.

"Peter's getting up, David. She's all right. Cheerful and very much her old self. She'll be down soon. Be nice to her. She deserves it."

"I know she does. She's wonderful and I've been a

fool. Thanks for all you've done, Trudie."

"Peter was my bridesmaid," was all she said.

John now stood at the entrance to the barn facing the others, who were grouped round the end of the table. Suddenly he gave them a stiff little bow.

"May I speak, if you please. I am very sorry for trouble caused and to thank David and Peter for saving my life yesterday. And to you all. And to Herr Ingles who took me to the hospital."

An awkward silence was broken by David who said:

"That's all right, John. We were all in a mess together. Do you think all that money was left under the tree by your father? And don't stand out there looking so uncomfortable. Come in and look at the loot. I suppose this was what you were looking for?"

John stepped across and fingered the notes. Then he said:

"I think this must have been what was hidden by my father. Some of you know that he told me in a letter that he would hide it if he was in danger. He told me also that I would never read the letter unless he was dead . . . But I did not find the money. Jenny did, and so, perhaps, in your country, the money belongs to her. If I had not been – what do you say – crazy for it? That is it. If I had not been crazy for it, I would not have been in the mine yesterday, when I would be dead perhaps but for Peter and David who saved me when they might have saved themselves first . . . I do not want the money now but what you do with it I do not know . . . Here is Peter. Ask her."

They all turned to see Peter standing on the threshold. What instinct had made her put on a skirt and a bright blue linen blouse only Trudie knew because she had lent her the blouse! She had never looked prettier.

THE TREASURE AT LAST

"Give the money to Mrs Clark to make her independent of Jem," she said. "You can fix it, Charles. I heard what John said. Tell her that you're not going to put the police on to Jem and then she can come back to the cottage. Even if she can't have the money, you'll tell her that you're not going to do anything to Jem, won't you? Oh, dear! Please don't all stare at me. Am I talking too much?"

Jenny and Mary hugged her, while Charles said:

"Somebody will have to tell the police about this find, I suppose, but I'm prepared to forget Jem Clark if he behaves himself in future. All right, Peter. I'll see Mrs Clark. I'll drive over to Shrewsbury and fix it."

"Peter's right," Trudie said. "Mrs Clark has suffered more than anybody else."

Mr Ingles nodded. "Seems sense to me. What about this lad John? What do we do with him?"

John said, "I go back to Germany. I make my life again there. I go and see my old uncle in Hamburg and tell him all. I have been a fool."

David walked over to Peter. "I've been a fool too," he said quietly. "Come out with me while they're talking to John. I've got a lot to say to you."

She began to protest, but he took her hand and led her across the farmyard and out through the sixth white gate into Jenny's "whispering wood".

"Where are we going?" she said breathlessly. "What's happened? You're rather peculiar all of a sudden."

"Splendid!" he said firmly. "I'm going to be peculiar from now on. Everything is different after yesterday."

"I can only remember some things about yesterday," she said. "You're hurting my fingers, David. Where are we going?"

"Where we can't be interrupted. This will do. Now what's all this about you and your father leaving

Hatchholt, and why were you so mad with me?"

They were in the heart of the wood now. She stood with her back against a tree and looked up at him. The only sound was the sighing of the wind in the branches and David was never to forget the sweet scent of the pine needles under their feet.

"Trudie told you about Daddy, I suppose. She'd no right to do that. None of the others know, but it's true. I'll tell you about it presently. I was angry with you because you were selfish and unkind. I sent you a wallet for Christmas and you never even thanked me."

"Of course I did. I wrote soon after Christmas and you never answered. I use the wallet every day."

"Oh, David. You really wrote? I thought you didn't like my present. Acksherley, as Mary says, I thought you were trying to show me that you'd sort of grown up there in London and had forgotten me — " Suddenly she was being kissed and when she recovered her breath and said, "David! You've never done that before," he kissed her again.

"That's a pity," he laughed. "I grew up yesterday, Peter. There's never been any girl but you, but I've been a fool not to tell you – and all this just because my letter never reached you. I wrote to Hatchholt and not to your school. I suppose it went astray in the post."

She told him then of her unhappiness over her father and how she hated the idea of moving. He told her that he was leaving school at the end of next term and for four months had been working desperately hard for his A-levels because his father wanted him to go to Oxford and that he was scared of disappointing him. He knew he should have written more often, but when he didn't hear from her he decided she didn't care! And he wrote to Jenny about this holiday because he was silly and proud. There was nothing new in what they said to each other. Nothing new in the way in which they mended a quarrel, and nothing new in the promises they made.

Presently they went back through the wood. John, with his rucksack on his back, was walking alone down the track. He stopped and looked at them for a long moment before he smiled.

Peter held out her hand. "Goodbye, John. Good luck."

"I know now why my father liked England," he said. "I thank you two again and wish you luck together. *Auf Wiedersehen.*"

He turned and walked out of their lives.

"I don't expect they teach you German at your school," David said, "but that could mean 'Till we meet again.' We shan't forget your handsome stranger's last words, Peter."